The Misha Plate

by
Jacqueline Opresnik

ISBN e-book 97809878063-2-1
ISBN book 97817774328-7-4

Cover design by Jacqueline Opresnik

For Sandy, who took the time
to read my first efforts and make
this book possible.

Other Books
by
Jacqueline Opresnik

How to Make Money Flowers
Package from the Past
In Search of Jeremy Griffin
The Grants of Maxwell Street
The Grants at War
The Hunt for William Williamson
Murder in the Asylum
Forgotten Past

Chapter 1

"Sam's been hurt, can you come up sooner?" asked Stephanie, in an almost whisper. "I'd welcome another pair of hands; we're starting to get busy."

Jennifer switched the phone to her right hand. This was the first time her sister had mentioned Sam being hurt. "Hurt? Hurt how?"

"He stepped into a trap on the trail." There was a pause as Sam entered the room, and when Jennifer had pressed her further Stephanie changed the subject. "I'm looking forward to seeing you. When do you think you can make it?" she asked in a more cheerful tone.

"I have a few things to arrange first so maybe tomorrow or Friday for sure."

"Something's not right here," Stephanie concluded in a whisper again. "Too many things are happening."

Her phone call was upsetting. Jennifer had wanted to go into more detail but instead just reassured her sister that she would try to leave the next day.

That was yesterday, and now, just past Grimsby the traffic up ahead suddenly halted. An accident at Stoney Creek had backed up the westbound traffic for a good five miles. It was too late to get off the highway and take the service road around the problem so Jennifer sat back, put the car into second and decided to make the best of an annoying set back.

It was a beautiful, clear, bright day. Jennifer pulled her long dark hair back and fastened it with a pewter clip. She glanced out at the calm waters of Lake Ontario, thankful that it wasn't too hot or humid. Gas

1

fumes and heat, tend to make everyone irritable and she tried not to think about the time she was wasting. She wondered what kind of things were happening at the lodge and was eager to see her sister. At last, the traffic was beginning to move again. Slowly cars and trucks made their way to the left two lanes skirting the collision that seemed to involve three vehicles. The melodious tune from the Nutcracker drew her attention from the accident to her cell phone laying on the car seat. "Hello."

It was Karl, two hours into her trip and he was already calling her for reassurance.

"Just make sure Williamson gets his designs by Monday." Leaving a week early with two clients waiting for designs had left Karl a little frazzled. "You'll be fine. Okay, see you in two weeks.

She glanced back into the rearview mirror and noticed a white car identical to hers in the passing lane. It inched forward slowly passing her. The occupant seemed just as interested in her car and seeing her gaze gave a friendly wave.

You didn't see too many fifteen-year-old Mustangs around. Owned by her aunt for 14 years Jennifer had inherited her favourite car just last year.

His was also in good condition. The only difference Jennifer could see was the red pin stripe along the side. Hers was the only one she had ever seen that had a green stripe indicating green interior. Jennifer smiled and returned the wave noticing that the driver was a good looking, tan-skinned blonde. For another ten minutes the cars took turns passing each other at a crawl speed like two snails racing. Finally, the road opened up and started to weed out the more powerful vehicles from the trucks and overly timid drivers. Several times the two white Mustangs took turns passing each other in a harmless flirtation until he waved a final goodbye before exiting the QEW at Guelph Line.

Traffic was heavy now but moving at a good pace. The time wasted at Stoney Creek had actually saved her from the worst of Toronto's rush hour and it wasn't long before Jennifer was heading north towards Barrie. The drive was direct now, no thinking about what lane to be in or which exit to take once she passed Barrie, just stay on number 11.

It wouldn't be long now. Jennifer was eager to see her sister. The phone call had upset Jennifer more than she wanted to admit. Stephanie had always been the strong, practical one, not easy to unsettle but hearing her voice betrayed a worry and fear Jennifer had never seen in her sister before. She realized now after Sam interrupted their conversation that Stephanie had tried to hide her feelings from her husband.

He reached across to the passenger side of the car and checked his location again with the directions on a small crumpled up piece of paper, then edged over to the right-hand lane preparing to exit the Queen Elizabeth Way; a highway that linked most small cities in the Niagara region of Ontario.

Up ahead was the name he'd been watching for - Niagara Street. The day was bright and warm giving the promise of a good summer and it seemed like a good time of day to avoid both traffic and line ups.

His eyes scanned both sides of the tree-edged street looking at the names of various stores and businesses until he came upon the one, he wanted. Good, there was only one other car in the parking lot and he knew he'd missed the lunch time lines. The owner of a new BMW gave him a disapproving look as the door of the faded blue Chrysler swung open a little too close. He smiled at the expression on the man's face then flicked the remains of a cigarette his way. He entered the small building and moving to the right, followed the path of purple ropes that led to the "next" sign.

"May I help you?" asked a voice from behind the counter. There were two women seated at either end of the counter, each with their own computer and monitor before them.

Mary Willis had just come back from lunch and was preparing her forms and pens around her ready to finish off the rest of the day. She looked up at the man approaching her section of the counter. He was tall, average build with unkempt sandy coloured hair, brown eyes and a day's growth of beard. Although he smiled at her, his eyes were piercing, expressionless as he spoke.

"I'd like to inquire about a personal licence plate."

Mary reached up and handed him a pen and a piece of paper. "Would you print it here, please." Hurriedly he printed large letters in determined strokes then passed the pen and paper back to her. He noticed he was making her feel uncomfortable now. That was good. He continued to stare at her intently while she took the paper and read it aloud. "MISHA. That shouldn't be a problem, it's an unusual name," she said assuredly. "Truck or car?" she inquired.

"Truck."

Mary turned to enter the request into the computer. Her hand slipped nervously and hit the N by mistake. She began again, then punched in enter. The computer screen blinked then flashed back a response. "I'm very sorry sir. That name is already gone."

His eyes narrowed as he continued to stare at her. "How could that be? I promised that name for my wife's birthday!" This was the fourth license bureau he had been to today and he was beginning to get agitated. He needed to find that license plate. He fought to keep his anger under control.

"Are you sure?" he persisted loudly, generating a look from the other attendant.

Mary Willis entered the name again. "No, I'm sorry. A man in Marten River already has that name and unless his plates are turned in for some reason ..." When she looked up from the computer to explain further options, he was gone.

She was making good time now. Orillia was up ahead and seemed to be the indicator that the north was upon you. The scent of pine was suddenly evident and the air felt cleaner. Three more hours should do it. Up ahead was a preferred gas station. Her gas guzzler needed food and it was time to indulge it. That was the only downside to driving a big engine classic.

Jennifer wondered if the Mustang twin was also gassing up. She thought about its driver and decided it was probably a good thing that the traffic hadn't been at a standstill. That type, although she seemed to gravitate toward them was usually trouble for her. Jason had been the last romantic endeavour. As good as he looked, he wasn't that reliable and sometimes drank too much which brought out a mean streak. Jennifer had ended that, months ago but was still getting pleading phone calls on his good days.

The summer day was slowly coming to an end. Reluctant to give way to night the sunset seemed to linger on more than usual, or maybe it was just that now Jennifer was taking the time to enjoy the evening. Up ahead was the sign she had been watching for -Marten River. A gravel road took her off the main highway for several miles before it would turn off to a smaller, narrower road that led to the lodge itself. It was getting darker now and for some reason Jennifer felt she'd driven too far. She went on a bit further then decided to turn around and go back. The Mustang went slowly along the gravel road as if it too was watching, looking for the sign. Jennifer had passed many roads coming in, all with signs posting names of cottagers but she had missed the Lodge's sign. Driving at dusk one had to be especially wary. This was the hour deer were most often seen on the roads, or sometimes driven out of the bush by black flies or mosquitoes, they would dash out unexpectedly any time of the day. It was starting to get humid but Jennifer decided she would rather be warm than be bitten by insects so she kept the window rolled up. It was times like this that she wished her car had air conditioning.

There it was! The sign, indicating the turn off. It was quite visible from this side but on the other she could see a tree branch that had snapped over and was obscuring the view from the road. She would remember to tell Sam about that tomorrow. The winding road brought memories of trips to cottages up north. Every year the family spent two weeks at a rented cottage. Jennifer had enjoyed the fishing and canoeing with her dad but Stephanie usually wanted to stay near the beach area and enjoy the water especially if there were paddle boats. It was many years ago since they had all gone on vacation together and driving along this bush lined winding road suddenly brought back those childhood moments. She wondered if there was a dump nearby where one could sit at dusk and observe bears as they casually roamed the area looking for discarded tidbits to eat.

This road had only two other exits leading to private cottages, one on a small lake north of the lodge. For ten more minutes now, the road was part of the Painted Rock Lodge and the land surrounding it, all part of their grounds on a lake that was virtually uninhabited. Only one other cottage existed and their entrance to the lake was further up the gravel road. The rest was crown land which gave the lake its isolated feeling.

The lodge itself was made up of twelve sprawling housekeeping cottages of various sizes and a main building that housed Sam and Stephanie's quarters, a dining room for those guests that opted for the food service, an office and a tuck shop area. Behind the main lodge were four small one-room buildings that housed the laundry and equipment and were sometimes used in a pinch for lodging.

It was difficult to see much in the dark but the smell of cooking and twinkling of porch lights amid tree branches told her that most of the cottages were occupied. She parked her car near the office in a space left next to

Sam's new truck. Its extended cab and box made it seem much longer than it actually was, but there was plenty of room to park her classic car. Stephanie was at the door to greet her, "Hi, you made good time. I didn't expect you until eight."

"Traffic wasn't bad once I got past Toronto, boy am I tired." Jennifer struggled through the door with an overstuffed suitcase. She had resisted the thought of bringing her computer, after all it was only a week's difference from her planned vacation. Everything was written out, planned for the next two weeks and at the last minute she had convinced herself that Karl could handle things until she returned.

It was nice to finally arrive. The smells of cooking made Jennifer hungry.

"Here, I'll take that, your room's down here at the end of the dining area." Jennifer looked around the dining room and hallway adjoining the office. It was different from her last visit. "We added this hall and doors into the laundry and this room" Stephanie indicated the renovated smaller room that used to be a part of the laundry building. Stephanie lifted the suitcase onto a wooden chair near the entrance of the small room then turned to give her sister a hug. "I'm so glad you're here."

Stephanie looked tired and stressed, and she gave Jennifer a weak smile as a voice came from the dining area.

"Is that my gorgeous sister-in-law?"

"Hi Sam, I'll be out in a minute."

"I saved supper for you," said Stephanie. Jennifer hadn't eaten since lunch and was appreciative that

Stephanie had thought to save something hot for her to eat.

Together they sat at one of the dining room tables after Jennifer had freshened up. Sam appeared in good spirits despite his infirmity and welcomed Jennifer with a big hug. "We're glad you're here. Your sister's been a nervous wreck waiting for you to arrive," he teased, giving Stephanie a look then smiled. His foot was wrapped in a wide bandage and raised up on a cushion to soften its rest on the chair in front of him which helped lessen the pain. He just seemed to take everything that had happened this last week in his stride. "Accidents happen," he had concluded. Sam had taken some pain medication and decided to go to bed early leaving Stephanie alone with Jennifer to catch up on current news and reminisce. Jennifer enjoyed her meal. Stephanie was a good cook and could always teach her something new in the kitchen. This was one area Stephanie wouldn't need help with. A man and woman walked gingerly past the dining room windows waving about their heads as they went.

"Are you booked up?" Jennifer inquired after a sip of coffee.

"Pretty much. We've been lucky this early in the season. Some of the cottagers are repeat visitors." Stephanie had mentioned little about the lodge up till now. It was getting late and the two had found themselves chatting for several hours, mostly about family, relationships and shared childhood memories, but now Jennifer wanted to hear more. "What's wrong, what's going on here?"

"It's nothing you can put your finger on. Little things really, that happen at the most inconvenient times."

This was the first Jennifer had heard about anything wrong with the lodge since Stephanie and Sam had bought it last year. "When did this start happening?" she asked.

"Everything was fine up until we started getting regular bookings, then problems with barbecues, septic tanks, motors, and finally Sam stepped in a trap while out in the woods last week."

"What does Sam say?"

Stephanie gave a resigned smiled, "Sam? He's in love with this place and just accepts things as minor setbacks."

"Sam's right, I'm sure it's just the rust of taking over a new business. It takes a while to get everything running smoothly." Jennifer saw her sister's face brighten with her optimism. "Besides I'm here now and I can help with whatever you need done." Jennifer began to stack her dishes.

"Thanks, Jen." Stephanie suddenly seemed happier. "Go, I'll do that, you've had a long day. Get some rest and we'll talk tomorrow."

Her bed was firm yet comfortable and the owl hooting outside her window didn't keep her from falling to sleep as soon as she nestled her head into the pillow.

Chapter 2

Smells of bacon cooking and coffee perking wafted into her bedroom from the kitchen through the dining room. Her room was small but had ensuite facilities which she was grateful for; not wanting to walk past any guests that might be in the dining room to reach the washroom that was available in the main lodge. She showered quickly leaving her hair to wash later in the evening and hurriedly dressed in a loose-fitting green top that matched her eyes and her favourite pair of jeans with the buttons down the sides.

Sam was in the dining room, sitting at a table with a young couple obviously ready to begin fishing at this early hour. Sam had a map out and was highlighting areas they might try first. The couple were about her age and if dressing appropriately could coax the fish out of the lake, they would have no problem. Designer labels flashed and the woman smiled at Jennifer as she fixed her hair just so beneath her legionnaire sun hat. Their gear alone must have cost a fortune. She remembered her dad looking at a reel like that one but two hundred dollars back then was absurd for a father of two and he contented himself with his old dependable equipment. It still caught fish.

"Well, good morning. It's time you were up." Sam gave her a big smile. He reached up to give her a long hug, then nodded toward the couple that had just left the room and who were now walking hand in hand down to their boat at the dock. "Nice couple. They just got married last week and are spending part of their honeymoon here. I don't think either one of them has been fishing before." He smiled to himself. "Well at least they look good. I suggested they hire a guide for a day. They'll like that. No worry about putting on bait or taking off fish and Tyler running the boat will leave their hands free." He smiled again, picturing the scene.

Jennifer had joined him at the table when Stephanie brought in their breakfast. There were no other guests coming in today and no one except the young couple had arranged for supper later that evening. From her place at the table Stephanie could see into the kitchen and called out to someone who had just come in the back door.

"It's on the counter Tyler. You'll enjoy this couple, they're really keen to go fishing." She returned his wave then went back to her bacon, eggs and pancakes.

Sam took a couple of gulps of coffee to wash down his last bite of food then addressed Jennifer. "I have a job for you. Unfortunately, it means driving to Sudbury." Sam outlined the errand that meant going to several stores that were holding various motor parts and plumbing supplies. Sam's injury made driving difficult so the individual orders had been sitting in stores waiting to be picked up since last week. Jennifer agreed and after writing down all the relevant information regarding roads, stores, and items, she decided upon one more washroom break and a jacket before setting out. Stephanie added a second list of grocery supplies and Jennifer knew this would be an all-day venture.

Oh well, she enjoyed driving and at least there would be no Toronto traffic, but there were of course construction delays. Northern highways always seemed to have detours or long line ups due to single lane traffic on newly poured asphalt roads. Jennifer was glad now that Sam had insisted on her taking the truck.

Its size was a little intimidating but it was easy to handle and after a few miles, Jennifer enjoyed the softer ride and being up high she could get a better view of the car line-ups.

It was six thirty before Jennifer found herself back on the gravel road heading home. It had been a long day but she had been successful in picking up everything needed. Her eyes searched the road watching for animals. To the left was a small clearing that stretched back off the road. She hadn't seen it yesterday. It would have been a pleasant place to have a picnic. Up ahead was the road cutting off to the lodge and she would make sure not to miss it this time. Her eyes flicked about the road taking in everything on this beautiful day. A heron flew low across the road with the promise of water nearby and she remembered the small pond she had seen last year on a walk with Sam and Stephanie as they proudly showed off their new home. A chipmunk dashed at an opportune time across the road, tail raised high in the air giving the illusion that he was running on tip toe.

She knew where the sign was now and slowed down a little to let on-coming traffic pass before turning. There was something strange about the car coming toward her. It didn't seem to want to turn yet slowed down also. Then suddenly the blue car accelerated toward her. For an instant Jennifer froze, thoughts rushing, deciding what to do.

The on-coming car grazed along the side of her door with a terrible sound as she turned the wheel frantically to the right, and Sam's truck, his beautiful new truck skidded sideways into the gravel ditch.

Jennifer's seat belt kept her from being buffeted within the cab and she held her breath as the sound of the vehicle passed.

Another sound. That of wheels skidding on gravel. A door slamming and a man's voice. She had turned off the engine by now and seemed aware of every little sound, her senses heightened by the recent event. A mosquito whined around her outstretched arm on the front seat. The clock on the dash; it's flickering sound as the number changed but she could not make out what the voice was saying. The truck was almost perpendicular to the road now. She leaned up unhooking her seat belt and grabbed on to the arm that was offered to her through the window.

"Are you alright?" he said loudly as if he had been asking the question repeatedly and she was refusing to answer.

"Yes, I think so. Thank you." Jennifer was shaking now. It seemed to take forever to get the door open.

"Did you hit your head on the steering wheel?" But Jennifer didn't answer. She was intent on checking the road around them. She had heard of accidents like this one where the perpetrator had circled back and pretended to be the helpful witness and rescuer. She sighed and closed her eyes. The vehicle behind her truck was a black station wagon.

"Thank you for stopping." she said and for the first time looked at her rescuer's face. His eyes searched her face and hair for signs of injury before his arms lifted her from the driver's seat. His hair was long and dark but well cut and styled back in a neat fashion away from his face. His nose although a bit large for his face, was straight and seemed to go with the intense steel blue eyes and angular facial features. A thin moustache followed the contour of his upper lip which gave his face an authoritative older look.

There was strength in the arms beneath the black jacket he wore as he carried Jennifer to a grassy area at the rear of the truck. "You were lucky." Then trying to reassure her he added, "The truck doesn't look too bad." He glanced into the back of the pickup truck. "Do you have a rope? The car's a 4x4. I could probably pull you out if we had a rope."

"Maybe in the back," she offered.

Opening up a rubber tub Sam always kept in the back for emergencies he found the necessary equipment then turned to Jennifer. "Do you know why he was trying to force you off the road?"

Jennifer was a little less shaken now and tried to replay the events in her mind. "No, I don't."

"I don't suppose you had time to see the licence plate number. I know I didn't, it all happened so fast." He suddenly stopped fishing out the length of rope he'd found in the box and sat down beside her.

"I'm sorry. I didn't ask you what you wanted to do. Do you live far from here? I could take you home first then help your husband pick up the truck." He took off his jacket that had concealed a muscular body beneath a short-sleeved shirt. Jennifer stared at him for a moment thinking, and realized that he showed genuine concern and probably feared she may have an after affect from the incident.

"Let's take it now, if you think we can pull it out. I know Sam will worry about the truck if I just leave it here."

He smiled at her realizing now that he didn't even know her name. "My name's Mike Kelly." He took her hand as the two stood up. "I'm staying at a cottage not too far from here."

"Jennifer Shea," she smiled. "I'm helping my sister and her husband Sam at their lodge for a few weeks."

The gravel ditch became deeper and narrower at the front of the truck. Mike Kelly completed tying the rope securely around the hitch. They'd have to pull it out backwards to avoid it from tipping over.

"It's too bad his license plate wasn't as easy to remember as this one." He tapped the back of the truck near a nicely framed personalized plate. "Who's Misha?"

Jennifer smiled as she remembered her sister's tabby cat. Misha had been a wonderful devoted pet. She explained how Sam had purchased the plate for her in memory of the friend she had lost to a raccoon attack their first spring here.

After reversing the position of the station wagon and securing the other end of the rope, Mike Kelly offered her his car keys. "Do you mind if I back the truck out?" he asked. "I'd feel awful if it tipped over with you inside."

"Well just this once. Maybe I'll get a chance to rescue you someday."

It didn't take long to get Sam's truck back on the road and soon they were travelling down the dirt road to

Painted Rock Lodge.   There was no real damage other than the scrape on the driver's side.

The light was on and someone seemed to be waiting at the door of the lodge office.   Mosquitoes buzzed around the entrance attracted by the light, as Jennifer and her rescuer climbed up the rock-slab steps and into the building. It was dark now and Jennifer could see that Stephanie seemed more anxious than she had ever seen her before. Sam had been sitting at the table with his leg resting on an adjacent chair but now he was up having noticed the long scrape on the side of his truck.

"I'm alright.   Really." she had explained after introducing Mike Kelly to her family.   Jennifer tried to describe the events of the afternoon as best she could. They shared some coffee as each offered up a motive for the attack while they waited for an OPP officer to arrive and make a report. It was around ten o'clock when this business was finished and Mike Kelly left to find his way along the forest roads to his cottage.

"He seems very nice."   Stephanie said as she cleared away the empty dishes.

"Ya, I guess. It was nice of him to stop and help."

Stephanie smiled at her sister's lack of interest. Her expression turned to concern again as she stopped what she was doing and listened to Sam's rhythmic uneven pace on the bedroom floor above.

Stephanie came and sat down again opposite her sister and managed a weak smile. Then she poured them each another cup of coffee. Stephanie looked good. A bit thinner since the last time they'd met but tanned and healthy looking. Her dark hair, shorter than Jennifer's but with the same thick straight deliberateness and bangs framing her brow, showed beginning streaks of grey.

"First Sam and now you." Her sister sounded mysterious again. She looked around the grounds through the screened windows of the porch before continuing as if the trees themselves were listening. "Be careful, Jen," she whispered, "I'm starting to get a bad feeling about all this and I don't want you getting hurt." Her tone and sudden seriousness gave Jennifer a slight chill.

"What do you mean hurt. I'm fine and besides..."

Stephanie cut her short ready to finally confide in her what she'd been thinking. "I don't mean that. I didn't tell you how I feel about Sam's accident. I think it was planned." Jennifer found herself leaning forward at the table as if that would make the meaning of what Stephanie said more plausible. "Sam has walked that same trail hundreds of times. Then all of a sudden, he steps into an old trap laying hidden across the path. An accident? That doesn't make sense."

Stephanie took a sip of coffee then glanced upwards noticing that Sam had stopped pacing and must now be resting. "I didn't want to tell you over the phone, but he could have lost his foot because of that rusty trap. He'd walked quite far before Tyler heard him calling, then we rushed him to town."

Jennifer hadn't met Tyler yet but Stephanie had mentioned him over the phone. He was a young man, a local Ojibwa, who helped out at the lodge and acted as a guide for guests that wanted that additional bit of help on fishing excursions. Tyler had worked for the previous owners and Stephanie and Sam had acquired his services when they took over the lodge. Mark and Ellen Semple had been eager to sell after some personal problems prevented them from staying north and they had highly recommended Tyler after the deal was set.

Jennifer gave her sister a reassuring smile. "Don't worry. I'm here to help." She took her sister's hand and gave it a slight squeeze. "I'm sure it's just a coincidence." But was it? She couldn't help sharing Stephanie's thoughts for a moment. She changed the subject. "Why don't we make a list of all the things that need to be done, then I can get a better idea of where to start tomorrow." The two spent another half an hour going over daily routines, booking procedures and renovation progress before Jennifer went to her room on the ground floor of the main building.

Lying in bed she replayed the day's events again. Running her vehicle off the road made no sense. Maybe someone had temporarily lost control of their car then too scared to admit it, had fled the scene. She was lucky someone like Mike Kelly has stopped to help. Who knows how long she might have sat in the truck before someone stopped.

Chapter 3

Jennifer had set her alarm for seven but the haunting calls of a loon woke her earlier than she had intended getting up on this second day of her working vacation. She hadn't slept long actually, maybe four hours, her mind still dwelling upon the incident yesterday. Night seems to enhance any situation but as she began her morning chores the attack seemed far away and detached from her new world here. There were things to do and two cottages to get ready for guests that would arrive after lunch. There were no breakfast guests to prepare for so Stephanie took advantage of this rare morning to sleep in for a few hours longer.

Jennifer grabbed a quick bite to eat; toast, juice, and coffee. Laundry was first on the agenda. The people in cottage four had left at dawn for a long trip back to Buffalo so she could start their first thing. They were a nice family of four, the two children not yet teens and they had left the cottage fairly clean.

Jennifer started by stripping the beds and replacing the linens. Then rather than vacuum she took the braided carpets out and hung them over the railing ready to beat for sand later, intending to damp mop on her return visit. The sun had burned off the morning mist quickly indicating the coming of a hot sunny day and Jennifer was thankful for this hot dry weather which made life difficult for the mosquito population.

The laundry room was central to the camp and attached to the main lodge and even though guests were required to bring their own towels, according to Stephanie there always seemed to be a load of laundry in progress.

Jennifer stuffed in two sets then prepared the disinfecting solution and supplies necessary to finish the job in number four.

It was nearly nine and the couple in number seven, a one-bedroom cottage past the boathouse, had started to pack their car. Sam who had been tied to the office area lately answering phones and helping Stephanie with guests, now found it necessary to spend more time at the neglected boathouse. There were three motors to repair and Sam liked to keep tabs on the workings of the boathouse.

Tyler had agreed to work more hours since Sam became injured but this morning, he was out on the lake with the honeymoon couple. Their previous day fishing trip had been a great success and Tyler's shore lunch was the highlight of their day.

Jennifer returned a wave goodbye as the couple in number seven left, and headed back over to number four to finish up the cleaning. Check out time was ten o'clock and Jennifer was glad that she would be able to get an early start on the cleaning.

Two chubby children attempted to play badminton in a grassy clearing near the lodge that had been set up with the necessary items needed to play horse shoes, croquet and badminton. In front of the clearing a sandy beach covered a large expanse before dipping gradually into the lake. A mother sat on one of the colourful wooden chairs at the lake's edge, half reading and half watching her young child splashing in the water.

Jennifer hadn't walked far when a truck pulling a fishing boat drove up the dirt road and stopped in front of the lodge next to the sign that said -Office.

Knowing Stephanie would still be in bed Jennifer set her cleaning supplies down and ran back past the young athletes to the office.

The driver got out slowly as if he'd been sitting for a long time and she could tell by the way he looked around that it was his first time here. Taking off his cap he wiped his forehead with his sleeve all in one motion. He smiled when he saw Jennifer coming toward them. "Hi. We've booked a cottage for the week." He threw his cap into the front seat of the truck. "I know we're early."

Jennifer smiled back and then realized that her gaze had focused on the man's friend. Suddenly feeling self-conscious she turned toward the office door and asked the driver to come inside and register.

Everything was laid out and straight forward. Guests filled in a card listing members of their party and addresses, then paid for their cottage and meal options if any. Docking fees applied for those with their own boats. Jennifer finished tallying up the bill then watched as the man paid with cash.

Jennifer tried not to look out the screened window at the green Explorer. The passenger was directly opposite her now, still sitting in the truck and appeared to be tired after a long trip.

Jennifer glanced down at the registration card. Glen Malloy and Derek Kerr from Ottawa. Both men seemed in their thirties. Glen Malloy a balding, round-faced, red-cheeked type and Derek Kerr a rugged, blonde, tan-skinned type.

Glen Malloy apologized again for arriving early and explained he expected that their accommodation probably wouldn't be ready yet. He seemed more at ease when Jennifer suggested that they take care of launching their boat and see Sam about docking arrangements. By that time, she assured him, their cottage would be ready. Jennifer directed him to the curve in the road behind the lodge that led to the ramp and boathouse area with its covered and uncovered docks.

Jennifer waited for the vehicle to move then quickly looked up number seven on the wall chart which told the number and kind of beds in each cottage so she could take the corresponding sheets with her when she went.

Number seven was a one bedroom with two double beds. It was the closest to the boathouse so she wouldn't have much time to run back and get her supplies then do everything necessary to make the cottage ready for its new occupants. The two chubby children had given up their strenuous game and seemed content now to make sand castles at the water's edge.

Twenty-five minutes later Jennifer came out to the porch with the last of the rugs to be shaken. The bathroom and bedroom were finished and she had just damp mopped the kitchen and living room areas. The last couple had taken their own garbage over to the recycle bin area and had left the cottage as they had found it.

Their boat secured at an assigned spot the two men began unloading their truck. Jennifer replaced the last of the rugs and met Derek Kerr on the porch coming in as she was going out. Her arms full she backed out of the screen door and hit him square on the knee with her broom handle. Before Jennifer could apologize, he had muttered some obscenity then laid down the case of beer he was carrying.

"I'm sorry." Jennifer winced an expression of sympathy. "Are you alright?"

He glanced up from rubbing his knee then looked at her for a moment. "Ya. It's okay." He waved off a call of help from his friend who was struggling with some large suitcases. "Are you going to tell me your name or just hit and run?" He smiled at his own humour and then offered his hand to Jennifer.

"I'm Derek." Glen Malloy found himself unloading the truck on his own and was unable to get his buddy's attention now that he had found a pretty girl to talk to.

Jennifer began to feel a little awkward and was still holding on to the rather heavy cleaning supplies while shaking Derek's hand. "Hi... Jennifer." After telling Derek her name she took back her hand and excused herself explaining she had more chores to do. She heard Derek laugh as she hurried back toward the main lodge and wondered if they were talking about her. She hoped she wouldn't have to speak to Derek for the rest of the week. There was something predatory about him and he made her feel uneasy. Glen Malloy seemed like a nice guy and she had supposed the same of his friend who now just seemed to be the good-looking, sleazy type. The thought gave her a chill and she continued past the lodge back up the same path to cottage number four.

By eleven Jennifer was working with Sam in the boathouse washing out the 18-foot cedar strip boats that would be used by the guests. Of the twelve boats used only six were rented as two guests came with their own boat and motor. Sam had repaired two of the three broken motors using parts Jennifer had picked up in Sudbury.

Three others had developed problems during the time he was laid up and would be next on the list of things to do.

The phone rang. He leaned back to reach the portable phone which Stephanie always carried with her strapped to her waist, but it was answered on the first ring from the office. "Well, looks like your sister's up." It was nearly noon and Sam knew that Stephanie would already have made the picnic lunches requested by the people in number two and eight and would have time now to feed her hungry co-workers.

From the shaded area in the boathouse Jennifer could see the patient parents of the two chubby children as they left their dock in one of the lodge boats. Their bulky life jackets made them appear even larger and Jennifer could see one of the children holding on to the picnic basket and she knew now who was in cottage two.

As they were leaving, Tyler was pulling into number nine's dock with the honeymoon couple. There was a strange silence among the couple and she noticed the young wife decline the hand offered by her husband and preferred to stumble on to the dock on her own, while Tyler, using the bailing bucket poured water into the front of the boat. He spoke to the husband for a minute then repositioned himself back at the motor and slowly backed away from their dock and proceeded to bring the boat over to the boathouse.

Jennifer stood up on the dock to keep her balance as the soft wake rocked the floating dock up and down. Tyler pulled up beside Jennifer as she offered to take the rope at the front of the boat. He climbed out and stood next to Jennifer. He was a few inches taller than her and a very attractive young man. Probably a couple of years younger than her with a stoic unlined expressionless face.

He shook his head looking at the mess in the front and middle of the boat. Sam hadn't moved but now he was curious, wondering what they were looking at.

"Not a good morning, Boss." Jennifer turned from them and went back to the last boat she was working on to get the mop. Tyler was a man of few words but she overheard the story and the occasional laugh from Sam.

The loving couple from yesterday, were no longer speaking to each other. He had accidentally dumped a whole container of four dozen worms over his wife's new outfit. She had had a bit too much sun yesterday even with her Legionnaire hat on and had become nauseous on the return trip and threw up all over the front of the boat not thinking to lean over the side. And to make matters worse the husband had dropped the string of fish they had caught when he offered to help pull them in from the side of the boat. Tyler felt sorry for the waste but equally sorry that their morning had ended on such a sour note especially after yesterday's success. Sam couldn't help laughing and Jennifer hoped the young couple couldn't hear them. Sam put his arm around Jennifer's shoulders and introduced her to Tyler.

Tyler gave her a faint smile and offered her his hand. It occurred to Jennifer that he probably didn't smile much. He seemed a very serious person. Jennifer helped Tyler clean out the boat while Sam headed back to the lodge for lunch. Tyler didn't talk much either but Jennifer did manage to find out a little about him by asking questions.

He lived on a nearby reserve with his grandmother. He was twenty-two and had been working at the lodge since he was eighteen. He knew the area very well but had only just started guiding this year at Sam's encouragement.

By the time Sam had washed up, Jennifer and Tyler were in the dining room ready to enjoy one of Stephanie's specialities.

There was a nervous tension about Stephanie. Sam didn't seem to notice but Jennifer did. She smiled, and commented on the usual things but Jennifer sensed an uneasiness. Jennifer tried to turn her mood and recounted the honeymooner's morning adventure.

"Ah, that's too bad," Stephanie laughed at Jennifer's supposed re-enactment, "maybe tomorrow will be better."

"If they're still talking to each other," added Sam.

Tyler actually laughed at one point during Jennifer's expanded retelling of the worm incident.

The rest of the afternoon wasn't any less hectic than the morning. Tyler busied himself by doing the garbage run. Collecting, sorting and disposing of the cottager's garbage took a few hours. Most people were helpful in that they sorted their recyclable items in the box provided on their porch and left their garbage bags tied and secured in a metal canister next to the box. There was the odd mess to clean up when a bag was left out on the porch overnight then ripped apart by raccoons or the occasional bear.

Sam had exhausted his energy for the day and went to lie down after taking some pain medication. Jennifer changed the linens in number two and was thankful that the family was staying for another week so she didn't have to clean out the cottage. Everything was done that needed to be done and Stephanie was now in the lodge looking after the office and tuck shop.

It was a quiet afternoon. The sun itself was very hot, but in the shade and with the light breeze it was a gorgeous day. Most of the cottagers had gone out earlier in the day and Jennifer could hear the far-off drone of a motor as it started then wound down to stop shortly after. She thought about joining Stephanie. It would give them a chance to talk on their own. Stephanie had just hung up the phone and was adding another name to her booking folder. "Mr. and Mrs. Collini, two bedroom, August 18th." Stephanie smiled at her sister. "How are you holding up so far?"

"Fine, I just stopped in for some of that iced tea you promised and to see if you needed help with anything." The iced tea was at the far end of the table away from Stephanie's paperwork so Jennifer helped herself then sat in a padded wicker chair next to Stephanie.

"Everything's caught up, finally. I'm glad you were able to come up early." Stephanie hesitated then gave her sister a sheepish look. "I must have sounded crazy on the phone. I don't know what you must have thought. I guess Sam's injury was the last straw and suddenly I was overwhelmed and convinced of a conspiracy." She closed her binder then picked up her cup of tea. "But everything seems fine now."

"It's been a tough, few weeks for you," agreed Jennifer, "no wonder you were stressed out." Jennifer finished her cool drink. "Anyway, you've got me for two weeks and I can always extend it for another if things get hectic."

Jennifer was glad her arrival had made a difference. It must have been difficult for Stephanie stuck at the lodge looking after the guests while Sam was injured. But now she seemed a lot better and Jennifer was eager to continue with her working vacation.

Cottages eleven and twelve were still being renovated and Jennifer decided to go over and see what condition they were in. She was handy with tools. Ever since she was little, she had helped her dad with projects around the house. She enjoyed the 'How To' programs on television and had acquired a great bit of know-how on things to do with renovation.

Number eleven was a two-bedroom cottage. The porch had been raised and levelled, sanded and stained a dark walnut colour. Inside the layout was similar to the cottage she had cleaned earlier only in reverse. She walked into the large room off the porch which was both kitchen and living room. At one end was a new gas fireplace which Sam had said was more economical than electric heaters and was safer than a wood fireplace. Eventually the other ten cottages would be equipped with this type of heating. The walls had been resurfaced in wide tongue and groove pine strips and had been lacquered with a clear finish. The rooms were empty of furniture ready for the floor to be finished.

Jennifer could see the boxes of tile sitting in the corner. The prepping of the floor had already been done and she knew this was a job she could tackle. The floor extended into a short hall midway from the room, with a bathroom at its end and two bedrooms exiting either side.

Jennifer checked the floors in these areas also and saw too that the nail holes had been puttied in and any irregularities in the wooden underlay had been seen to.

There was a box of tools sitting in the corner and Jennifer was able to find what she needed without going back to the lodge. A measuring tape, a square, a yardstick and a pencil were the things she needed and she would make do with the scissors for any cutting that had to be done. After measuring the room from corner to corner diagonally she discovered the room was almost square so it wouldn't take much planning in order to start.

Two hours later the room was done and there were still enough tile boxes left which told her that the whole cottage would be done in the same tile. It was inexpensive tile, the kind you peel and stick but the colour and design Stephanie had chosen made all the difference and the room looked beautiful.

The bathroom fixtures were in and would require a great deal of tile cutting and fitting. Jennifer decided to leave this for later and for now work on the two bedrooms. Both were unusually square and it was as if someone knew she would be using tile and made the floor size according to the tile measurement. It didn't take long and as she finished up the last room Jennifer could hear Stephanie ring the brass bell that hung outside the lodge entrance to the dining room.

The four ate in the dining room with guests from cottages ten and eight. The woman who had earlier sat by the water's edge watching her young child now sat at a table for four with her child, husband and brother-in-law. Six people sat opposite them, three couples from cottage eight. Sam was adjacent to the table of six and listened intently as one of the men told him of their day's excursion to the far end of the lake. Up by the small falls that fed the lake at the furthest end he had caught a twenty-inch pickerel and his friend had something on the line that was so big it broke the line after its initial hit and took the lure with it.

"Did you have a steel leader on?" asked Sam.

"No," admitted the other man, "I actually wasn't prepared to catch something that large near the falls."

Pike had teeth, and a large one could easily cut your line. "But I'll be ready for it tomorrow," he said with a laugh.

The brother-in-law at the next table, having overheard the fish story asked the three how to get to the falls. Everyone seemed excited at the prospect of catching that big one. Sam was also happy to hear that the three fishermen, unless having a special fish dinner, usually released their catches.

Jennifer helped Stephanie serve before joining Sam and Tyler. Tyler didn't often stay for supper at the lodge but tomorrow he would be taking a group out early for a day's guiding so for tonight he would use his usual one room cabin at the rear of the lodge.

The roast beef was delicious and after helping Stephanie with the dishes, Jennifer decided to relax and take a canoe for a short ride along the shore. There was still light and most of those out fishing since late afternoon would return shortly after dark. The water was still, not so much as a ripple. Jennifer chose the more manoeuvrable red canoe and leaving the beach area, went right past the boathouse along a tree-lined shore. She skirted the docks for cottages nine and ten and could see the occupants of cottage nine sitting on the porch holding hands. The honeymoon couple were obviously talking to each other again and she smiled at the thought of their morning mishap. She passed quietly by, her paddle dipping without a splash.

Past the two cottages being renovated she followed further along the shore as the land curved back into a bay-like depression. Trees along the edge had not been thinned as they had along the lodge's shore and the water's edge was over grown with wild rice and laden with tree branches and drift wood. Her canoe, leaning to one side as she paddled made a swishing sound as it flattened the rice in its path. It had been many years since Jennifer had been in a canoe and even though she was exhausted she was enjoying the calm water and gliding motion.

Up ahead Jennifer could hear some splashing near the shore beyond her view. She supposed it was an animal wading at the shore or a fish jumping while feeding on smaller fish in the shallow water. She wished now that she'd taken a fishing rod. Cedar trees stretched out over the water and as she manoeuvred her canoe around their branches, the source of the splashing sound came into view.

Mike Kelly had his hands full. He was knee deep in water and looked as if he was wrestling with a duck. He hadn't noticed Jennifer yet so she lightly tapped her paddle on the side of her canoe which made him look up. He smiled when he saw her sitting not ten feet away amused by his predicament.

"Well just don't sit there! I need some rescuing, or rather this duck does."

As she paddled on Jennifer could see that Mike Kelly had caught a wild duck in a large fishing net and was having a difficult time trying to hold it while he adjusted pliers in his other hand. Jennifer climbed out of the canoe into two feet of water and pushed the vessel up on to the rice stalks. She noticed now that the duck had a fishing lure embedded in its bill and fishing line wrapped around its leg, and she let out a sympathetic moan.

"What can I do?"

"Here, you take the net." Mike Kelly handed her the handle while he used one hand to steady the duck then the other hand armed with needle nosed pliers extracted the hook from the bird's bill. Jennifer wondered if the bird could feel pain in this area and she hoped not as he gave the lure a final twisted pull. The pliers had a cutting edge and Mike Kelly was able to cut and unwrap the line around the bird's leg.

Jennifer held the net firm and watched as this man gently helped the duck and then motioned for her to lower the net as he let the bird frantically escape into the water.

He looked younger than he did the day of the attack. His hair now wet was hanging shoulder length down the sides of a face that showed the excitement of a child.

"I'm glad you came by." He took the net from Jennifer then held her arm as the two waded out of the warm water into the cool night air.

"This is your cottage?"

"For the summer. It belongs to a friend of mine." Together they pulled the canoe up further on to the shore then he collapsed on the sand a smile of satisfaction beamed across his face. "I've been watching that duck since early this morning."

Jennifer sat down opposite him and crossed her legs tucking her bare feet into the soft sand. She smiled at his exuberance. "What made you want to catch it?" Jennifer pulled at her wet clinging clothes. The sky displayed every combination of red and blue now and soon it would be dark.

Mike Kelly sat up and combed his hair back with his fingers. "I don't know. She had seven ducklings and all day they've been hanging around the dock while I was working, as if waiting for me to do something." He looked directly into Jennifer's eyes. "I'm glad you came by though. I couldn't have done it by myself."

Jennifer smiled, glad now that she had gone for her canoe ride. She found herself staring at this man who seemed so different from the one she had met two days earlier. Maybe it was his unkempt appearance; the wet blue jeans and tank top, a day's growth of whiskers and the uncombed hair, she wasn't sure. He seemed to suit this environment; sandy shore, the woods, and a log cabin in the background. She could picture him as a hero in a wilderness movie. Jennifer didn't notice the first of the fishing boats returning, their motors winding down as they approached their dock.

Jennifer was deep in thought and didn't hear him the first time. "I was going to start a fire and cook supper shortly. Have you eaten yet?"

Jennifer saw that a camp fire had been prepared in a place that was obviously used for this purpose, a large stone outcrop at the edge of the water to the left of them.

"Yes, with the guests before I went out, but thank you."

Mike Kelly helped her up and this time she was aware of his hand surrounding hers and it made her shiver, or maybe it was just the cool night air.

Chapter 4

It was dark when Jennifer got back to the lodge. All but one of the lodge's boats had returned from fishing and Sam would keep watch from the office window until the last boat from cottage ten was safely tied up at the dock.

A flood light from a top a tree, placed so it would light up the docking area and beach had come on automatically now and would help guide the remaining boat home.

Jennifer had changed into her favourite jeans with the buttons down the side and a green flannel shirt. There were tables and chairs as well as the typical office furniture and Sam was sitting in his usual chair with his leg raised keeping the two of them company as Stephanie caught up on book work and bills. Stephanie had only smiled when Jennifer told her and Sam about their next-door neighbour and the duck. Being a man who loved nature, Sam had appreciated the rescue.

Among the pile of bills was one that should have had a zero balance. "Did you use your Visa card lately?"

"No. Just that one time in the States at the show. But that was back in February." Stephanie handed Sam the statement.

"Is it the same garage?" asked Stephanie.

The name of the business was the same and the amount owed was the same translated into Canadian dollars. It had been a stormy night in Pennsylvania at the yearly Sportsman's show where Sam had had a booth set up offering information about Painted Rock Lodge. Sam's truck had needed some minor repair and Rensen's garage had been the closest to the convention centre. The mechanic owner had been very obliging and had even offered Sam a ride back to the show. The truck was ready the next morning and Sam had paid by using his credit card. That was four months ago.

He passed the statement back to Stephanie. "I wonder why it took so long to go through?"

Just then the sound of a motor winding down and twinkling lights on the water told Sam that number ten was back and he could relax.

Through the screen the smell of a wood fire told Jennifer that Mike was preparing supper. She wished now that she had lied about dinner and stayed a little longer. The thought of him sitting on the beach after the rescue made her smile.

The smell of smoke grew stronger now and from her vantage point next to Sam she could see Glen Malloy and Derek Kerr outside their cottage. She touched Sam's shoulder as she went by. "Sam! Look!"

Glen Malloy was coughing, fanning the air and rubbing his eyes, and Derek was running toward the office lights. Smoke clouded the front porch and continued to billow from the cottage door.

Derek passed Jennifer on the steps of the lodge. "It's the fireplace! It started smoking!"

Tyler had heard the commotion and was running from his cabin to number seven. There were external taps at the side of all porches each with a long hose coiled under the deck for just such an emergency. But entering the cottage was impossible. There was little smoke coming from the chimney which indicated that there was a blockage in the pipe somewhere or the cottagers had forgotten to open the damper.

By now many of the other nearest cottagers were outside. Most were calm and just watched realizing that someone was taking care of the problem. One of the men from cottage ten helped Tyler pull the ladder out from under the lodge. The honeymoon wife was comforting Glen Malloy while he explained what happened and Sam stood next to Derek Kerr and watched. Jennifer helped guide the hose for Tyler as he climbed up beside the chimney and sprayed water down the fireplace pipe.

Another billow of smoke puffed from the cottage but eventually the smoke from the fireplace dissipated into the darkness of the night. Stephanie was standing on the steps of the lodge with cottagers from number two and six.

The two chubby children were excited and Jennifer could hear their voices in the dark. "Is there going to be a forest fire, mom? What about our cottage?"

Sam waved an arm to get her attention. "Call the fire tower and let them know it's only a smoking fireplace."

Stephanie went back inside to notify the authorities that there wasn't a fire at their camp. It had been a hot dry June so far and rangers would be extra alert to a cloud of smoke exiting from a forested area.

Jennifer held the ladder again for Tyler as he came down from the roof of cottage seven.

"There's something in the pipe." he said, satisfied that the blockage had caused the smoke backup. "Probably a bird or small animal."

Next to Sam, Derek's arms were animated now. "What about our clothes? "We can't sleep in there tonight!"

Sam tried to console his guest. "We'll move you over to cottage three tonight. You can get the rest of your things later. If you haven't eaten yet, come over to the lodge and Stephanie will fix you something." Derek seemed a little less upset now by the offer and went to talk to his friend about the new arrangements.

Sam waved to Tyler. "Keep everything open. Let's try to get it aired out in the next hour."

Tyler waved acknowledgement and then thanked Jennifer for her help. He placed the ladder along the back of the cottage while Jennifer rewound the hose and placed it back in its spot under the deck. "I'll have to unplug the chimney tomorrow," he said, "for now, we can open up the windows and check for any water on the floor."

Tyler started on the windows while Jennifer went back to the lodge to get a sponge mop and bucket.

Once the cottage was sufficiently aired out Jennifer helped Tyler move the guests' belongings over to number three. It was a two bedroom and had been cleaned ready for guests the day before she arrived. Glen Malloy came along and helped. They had eaten earlier before the fireplace incident but Derek was taking Sam up on his offer and having a hot roast beef sandwich in the dining room.

Moving was easier than she thought. Most of the men's belongings had not been taken out of the suitcases yet and it was really only some of the food from the refrigerator that had to be re-packed. Glen Malloy took a box from Jennifer's arms. "I'm sorry for all this bother," he said. "We didn't need to move. Our clothes are fine, and you can't smell any smoke now."

Jennifer liked Glen Malloy. He seemed a kind and considerate man not the type who'd have a friend like Derek Kerr. She could tell he was embarrassed by Derek's behaviour. "We're just co-workers," he explained as if reading her thoughts.

Water damage was minimal. Just the area in front of the fireplace was wet. Tyler had mopped up most of the water earlier so as not to cause the tiles to lift. She would work on the rest of the cleaning tomorrow.

The sound of wheels on a dirt road caught Jennifer's attention and she could see the late arrivals for cottage four stop at the office sign. The father of three young children got out slowly and closed his car door gently obviously not wanting to wake his small passengers.

Stephanie greeted him at the door and the driver went inside to register. Jennifer wondered why they were so late and found out later that they had been delayed at the Windsor border and by road construction along the way. That coupled with three young children who needed frequent pit stops doubled the time of their journey.

But now they were here and could enjoy the next two weeks without having to think about the trip back too soon. Because the children were young, Stephanie decided to give them cottage five instead. It had three bedrooms and was much nearer the beach area and would be vacant for the first week. The father looked tired but glad to be here.

Jennifer had left Glen Malloy back in number three now unpacking the perishables. When she reached the lodge office, she offered to show the new family to their cottage and explain some of the lodge routines regarding garbage and parking and where to get their boat in the morning.

It was nearly nine thirty now and as she walked back to the office to sit with Sam and Stephanie for a while and share a cup of coffee, she passed Derek Kerr making his way over to number three. As he went by, he smiled. "Has my partner moved everything over yet?" Then he laughed.

Jennifer didn't answer him and just walked faster. What a creep, she thought.

The evening air was warm and this was really the first time Jennifer had noticed the stars in the sky. Millions more than you could ever see from the city. A shooting star fell in an arc over the lodge then faded into the dark. She could see Sam and Stephanie at the office table. They were talking quietly and seemed to be waiting for her to come back inside. An owl hooted, probably the same one who sat outside her bedroom window her first night here. Jennifer's eyes glanced along the side of the lodge. She thought she heard something near the back of the building and decided to walk faster just in case it was a skunk or porcupine.

Stephanie held up a hot cup of coffee to her as she came through the door and Jennifer collapsed in a chair next to her sister. "Well, that was a bit of excitement. I'm exhausted." She sipped some of her drink. "And that Derek," she was whispering now realizing that voices carried at night, "what a jerk."

Sam gave her an amused smile. "Well at least you're not his fishing companion for the week, poor Mr. Malloy." The three of them chuckled at the thought.

Sam looked toward number three. "Where's Tyler?"

"I don't know." Jennifer looked around the lodge yard. "I guess he went back to his cabin. He's got an early morning."

Sam leaned back in his chair. "I'm glad he was here tonight. Things might have been worse if he hadn't used the hose right away."

Sam looked tired. He was a few years older than her sister and Jennifer had always thought of him as a distinguished older man. His sandy brown hair was swept over to the right of his face and it was difficult to tell if he had any grey hair. There was a tiny scar that crept from his left cheek down to hide in a full moustache, yet almost disappeared when he smiled. His brown eyes betrayed the stress of the long day. Jennifer liked Sam. He was a hardworking, good, kind man and he was mad about Stephanie.

The phone interrupted her thoughts. Stephanie checked her bookings folder and described the available cottage to a former guest on the phone. After switching the family of five there was only a two-bedroom cottage left, number four. The caller seemed agreeable and Stephanie entered his name in her book. "And that's six days total? We'll expect you tomorrow then. Goodbye."

Stephanie brought her folder to the table. "That was Mr. Nelson who was here two weeks last summer. He has had unexpected company from England and was delighted that there was room for them." She took another sip of coffee. "Do we have another boat and motor ready?"

Sam didn't hear her. His pain medication was adding to his exhaustion and he could barely keep his head from nodding. "Goodnight girls. I've got to go to bed."

Sam left and Jennifer switched to his chair so she was facing Stephanie. "I think he finished two this morning using the new parts, and the boats are all clean and ready to go."

Together they outlined the work for tomorrow. First thing would be to clean number seven so that Glen Malloy and his co-worker could move back in. Their current shelter could be cleaned later as the new quests weren't expected until Wednesday. Jennifer told her sister about the floor in number eleven and her plans to complete the job tomorrow. Stephanie looked down into her coffee and smiled. "Do you remember the summer we spent finishing Uncle Terry's cottage?"

"I don't think I'll ever forget those two months." Together the two teenage sisters had travelled up north in Stephanie's old Rambler. It wouldn't go more than 55 miles an hour so they had travelled at their own pace letting others pass if they wanted. Uncle Terry's cottage was just past Bancroft and had been built the summer before on a beautiful lake. The cottage was roughly finished, with no walls or ceiling and just underlay on the floor area. He had agreed to let the girls have the cottage for the summer if they did the work and finished the inside. Tools and most of the materials were waiting for them when they arrived.

Jennifer laughed as she remembered one particular incident. "Do you remember the morning they delivered the bags of fibreglass insulation?" They had developed a routine of working until all hours of the night often until two or three in the morning, then they would sleep in until almost noon and watch a snowy television screen while making pizza for breakfast.

This particular morning the delivery truck had delivered all the bags of insulation for the cottage. It was around eight in the morning and the two girls had acknowledged the order then went back to bed. Shortly after, it had started to rain, just a soft pattering you could hear on the brown paper bags covering the fibreglass. Neither had thought much about it until they heard a loud "poofing" sound.

Stephanie started to laugh. "Did we move fast. Out in the rain in our pajamas dragging in bags of wet fiberglass that were popping open like milkweed plants."

"But it was fun. I can't imagine what our parents must have been thinking. I know there were other cottagers around on the weekends, but two girls alone in the woods for two months with power tools. I wouldn't let my daughter go."

Jennifer suddenly looked excited. "Hey, it's still early, how about a swim? Out in the lake like we did at the cottage." They would often take a boat out beyond the sandy beach and swim at dusk when the water was as smooth as glass. Both had this thing about their feet touching the bottom of the lake and feeling who knows what.

Stephanie looked at her younger sister. It seemed a long time ago. A time when they had bonded as friends and discovered how much alike they were.

Uncle Terry was amazed when he saw the completed job. It had taken them longer than a work crew but every cross joint in the ceiling tile was perfectly aligned, every panelling joint trimmed so it was flush with the adjacent board. It had been a good summer.

"Let's go!"

Chapter 5

Sunday should have been a day of rest, but at a lodge there is always something that needs to be done or guests that require help in some way.

Tyler had left at seven with the couple and her father from cottage six. It would be an all-day fishing trip with a shore lunch at noon.

Sam was still asleep when Jennifer woke at eight but Stephanie had been up for a couple of hours already making the shore lunch preparations for Tyler and fixing breakfast for the honeymoon couple, and the couple and brother-in-law from number ten. "Morning, Jen. Have a seat." called Stephanie, "You might as well have breakfast with the others." The honeymoon couple were just approaching the dining room door as Jen made herself comfortable at a smaller table nearer the kitchen door intending to help Stephanie with the serving.

Mr. Newlywed pulled the chair out for his adoring Rachel and the two sat holding hands until the family from number ten arrived and sat at an adjacent table. There was talk of the previous night's excitement and speculation as to how a raccoon would get stuck in a chimney of that size monopolized the breakfast conversation. The brother-in-law from number ten commented on just such an incident a few years ago at his friend's cottage and explained to the novice couple that things like that did happen from time to time.

Halfway through breakfast Sam joined the group. Choosing to sit at a table near both parties Sam steered the conversation away from the chimney incident by asking them about their fishing plans for the day. The

Newlyweds had planned to go to town and look around. Stephanie had told Rachel about a craft shop and boutique just past the gas station that specialized in sporting outfits.

The mother and small child would spend most of their day at the beach area while the two men would try their luck up by the falls. Afterwards the brother-in-law would baby-sit while the couple had a chance to fish together later in the afternoon.

Stephanie joined Jennifer at the table for two after her guests had been served and together, they nibbled on strips of bacon with toast and coffee. Jennifer was sure now that Sam had convinced Stephanie the smoking chimney was just one of those things, so Jennifer had thought better than to bring up the subject again. Instead, she focused the conversation on the day's chores.

After a bite to eat with Stephanie, Jennifer went to prepare number seven for the two displaced cottagers now residing in cottage three. As she passed the boathouse, Derek gave her an eager good morning from Glen Malloy's boat as it sat tied to number seven's dock, rocking gently.

Jennifer was obligated in returning the greeting and before she could turn to continue up the path to number seven Derek flashed a triumphant smile and sprang to the dock from the flat fishing platform at the bow of the boat.

"I didn't get a chance to thank you for last night," he said, "For helping Glen and me with our belongings." He smiled again as if that would make up for his lack of consideration.

Something about him annoyed Jennifer. Maybe it was his arrogant confidence in himself and good looks or maybe the way he behaved towards Glen Malloy but she tried to be polite.

"I hope you have a good day fishing," she said flatly intending to carry on up the path. "Mr. Malloy seems very enthusiastic to be here," she concluded.

"Yes," said Derek quickly, seeing a way now to keep the conversation going. "He just lost his wife last month," When Jennifer looked concerned, he laughed, "Oh no, I mean he got divorced." He waited for a laugh in response from Jennifer which didn't come then continued, "He doesn't have too many friends so I offered to come up with him for the week." Hoping he had scored some points he smiled again then moved to block Jennifer's way to the cottage.

Glen Malloy offered a greeting as he came past the boathouse carrying their gear for the days fishing and joined them. He smiled at Derek's persistence then gave Jennifer a knowing smile.

"Well, are we ready to go?" he suggested to Derek, giving Jennifer the opportunity to end her conversation with Derek.

Finding no other reason to pursue his discussion he took the jacket Glen offered him and made his way back to the boat.

"I hope he hasn't been bothering you too much," he said in a low voice. "He's harmless really."

Jennifer smiled, "That's alright. Your cottage will be ready by the time you get back."

"Thank you, our gear is sitting by the door on the porch. There're just a few things in the fridge. We can get them later," he suggested.

"If you like, I'll have everything brought back for you," offered Jennifer.

"That's kind of you, thanks." He smiled a goodbye then joined a waiting, Derek.

The cottage wasn't too bad. The rooms had been aired out since the night before and all that was really necessary was to change the bedding and damp mop the living room area. Tyler had taken care of removing the dead animal from the pipe earlier that morning and the two guests should have no further problems with the fireplace for the rest of their stay.

On her way back to the lodge Jennifer could hear that the kids in cottage five were up and ready to start their vacation. She wondered if their father had been down to the boathouse yet and having found no one there had returned to the cottage disappointed. The boats were ready it was just a matter of choosing one and assigning a dock number.

Jennifer decided to bring one from the boathouse and set it up at the dock ready for the family of five. The boathouse was darker this time of the morning, with the opening facing south west it would take another three or four hours before light would filter in through the front entrance.

Jennifer chose the boat at the end of the dock as it would be the easiest to back out and turn around. The gas tank was full and she squeezed the rubber ball on the fuel line before starting the motor. Each boat had a fifteen-horse motor, similar to the kind her father had. After setting the handle to neutral she pulled the cord. Nothing happened. She tried again but it wouldn't start. After several attempts Jennifer abandoned that boat and tried the one tied in front of it. Both of these motors had been repaired the day before and should have started just as easily as they had after Sam had worked on them, but they wouldn't.

Tyler had taken the guide boat, leaving the boat and motor from number six free for the day. Jennifer decided to take that boat for now and arrange for a switch later on in the day after Sam had a chance to go over the motors and figure out what was wrong. She took the path that led along the shore back towards the lodge and number six at the edge of the beach. The boat was clean and any fishing gear that was usually left in overnight had been taken now for the days trip with Tyler. Jennifer sat at the back of the boat and tried the motor before untying the front. It started on the first try. Leaving it in neutral she untied the two ropes at either end of the boat then slowly started back towards the boathouse. There was half a tank of gas left in this gas tank so she would switch it for a full one first before delivering it to cottage five and then label this one for cottage six and change it back later. Guests paid for their gas and it wouldn't be fair to start the new guests off with less than a full tank.

As Jennifer pulled up to the dock at number five the father and two of his children greeted her. They seemed close to six years old and Jennifer could see now that the boy and girl were twins. Their father caught the rope she tossed and helped pull in the front to be tied. Along with a full tank of gas, Jennifer had remembered to bring five life jackets. Their mother was joining the group now with a slightly younger child and Jennifer was glad now that she had prepared a boat for them. The family was obviously intent on taking a ride.

After speaking with the father, Bob Tokar, Jennifer could tell that he had been around boats before and knew how to handle the motor. She watched as the father placed his children in various seats and explained the rules to them.

Each had on one of the smaller life jackets Jennifer had brought and waited excitedly for their father to start the motor. Jennifer was holding the front rope now.

"Here! I almost forgot." She pulled a folded piece of paper from her pocket and handed it to Mr. Tokar. "It's a map of the lake. It shows the rocky areas and the depths of various locations." She remembered Sam's description of the lake from the wall map in the lodge. "About half a mile to our left is a quiet bay with a large flat outcrop." She noticed the thermal bag his wife had brought with her from the cottage. "It's a nice place for a picnic."

The younger child wiggled on the seat next to his mother and shouted, "A picnic! A picnic!"

"Thank you. And thank you for bringing the boat over." With the map safely tucked away in his jacket pocket the family of five were off on an adventure. Jennifer liked Bob Tokar. He was obviously a good father and he and his wife seemed to have their parenting skills on the same wavelength. It was a beautiful morning, not too cool and she was sure the children would have a great time.

Back at the lodge the breakfast crowd was leaving. Some guests had been out on the lake for two or three hours already and would be coming back soon for their mid-morning meal, while others like the couples in nine and ten took a more leisurely approach to fishing and didn't really care what time of day they went out as long as the weather was nice. The three ladies from cottage eight were obviously not as enthused about fishing as their husbands. Jennifer could see them out on their dock preparing the wooden surface for sunbathing. Towel, pillows, bottles of suntan lotion and refreshments. She could hear them giggling about something one of them had just said and knew they were enjoying this time alone away from the men.

Jennifer wondered if the couple from number two and their two chubby kids were up yet but she couldn't see their dock from the beach. They didn't seem to be the avid fishermen type either, but like many people they probably enjoyed just being away from the city.

With her cleaning done Jennifer decided to keep her promise and move number three's contents back to Glen and Derek's cottage. It was a fair walk between the two and Jennifer decided in case their bags were heavy, to drive her hatch back over to three and load up rather than struggle walking the distance. It was up on the hill and like cottages one through four had a small driveway.

Sam had finished his breakfast and was getting an extra paper map from a pile kept in the office for guests. The brother-in-law thanked him. "It looks like a good day for fishing," he said. "Just enough cloud."

"You may want to take an extra tank with you," suggested Sam. "It's a fair distance to the end of the lake. Help yourself to a tank in the boathouse. There's a book there to enter your name and tank number." The brother-in-law thanked him again and joined his waiting fishing partner.

Jennifer greeted Sam at the front of the office after parking her car. "It's nice to see you're walking a little better."

Sam smiled back. "Well let's hope it lasts a while today." The bandage was off now and Jennifer could see the healing wound above his ankle and she cringed at the thought. "Listen." He locked his arm around hers. "Are you up for another trip to town?"

"Before you lose your only helper today you better know something first." Jennifer started them along the path to the boathouse.

"And what is that, my dear sister-in-law."

"The motors you fixed yesterday won't start." Jennifer explained the problem she had earlier in the morning and her solution as they walked.

Jennifer helped Sam into the last boat tied up to the boathouse dock. "I'm glad you thought of switching boats. I'm sure they won't mind as long as someone else isn't using their gas." He prepared the motor as Jennifer had done and pulled the cord, but it wouldn't start. He tried three more times and then stopped. "I don't understand, they both worked fine yesterday." Sam looked concerned now. "You say the other one is the same."

"Maybe you better try it," said Jennifer, "maybe I didn't do it right. They could be flooded."

With Jennifer's help Sam sat at the back of the next boat and tried to start the motor. "I don't smell any gas. The tanks are full. It's not flooded, but something's wrong."

Together they pulled the boats over to the work area where Sam could reach the motors easier from a smaller U-shaped dock. "Speaking of gas, that was the favour I wanted you to do. Go into town and fill the larger tanks for me."

The lodge did not have its own gas pump yet, so every so often Sam would go into town and fill up the many tanks he kept in the boathouse. Guests would then pay for each tank of gas they used during their stay.

"Stephanie wants to go too. The Tuck shop is closed till noon and I think she needs a break."

Jennifer agreed. "What about Mr. Nelson? He might arrive before we get back."

She could see the frustration on Sam's face and she knew he didn't need any more problems right now. "I'll put a note on the office door. If they arrive early, they can find you here. I'll bring back the portable phone for you."

Sam gave her a tired smile in return. "Have I told you yet, I'm glad you're here."

"Yes, several times." Jennifer said warmly. "I'll be right back."

It was just after ten when Jennifer picked Stephanie up at the office after loading on the empty gas tanks. The tuck shop was closed for now and there was a sign on the door referring guests to the boathouse.

The town wasn't far and if there was time, they would check out the local craft shop. Back down the dirt road to the gravel road intersection Jennifer was beginning to recall some of the woodland landmarks along the way. A large pink granite rock would be jutting out at the next curve, a dead pine with one branch sticking out horizontally like an arm pointing, a clearing near the edge of a small bog like area. "This is a job I hate," confessed Stephanie, "I'm glad you're driving. I get so nervous with gas tanks piled up in the back."

Jennifer remembered how nervous Stephanie used to be especially driving past Toronto. Once returning from Haliburton for the first time on their own they had been confused by the highway signs. One said Toronto and one said Hamilton. Not wanting to go to either place they had ended up at the Canadian National Exhibition in Toronto by mistake and took forever to get back on track to Niagara. Stephanie was the oldest and having her licence first it was up to her to drive if the girls were to go anywhere on their own. But Jennifer enjoyed driving and was glad of this opportunity to chauffeur her sister around.

The branch that had hidden the sign at the turn off was now cut back leaving the lodge sign visible for the new guests finding their way for the first time.

As Jennifer pulled to a stop before turning toward the town, she felt the pedal slip a little. There was something not right. Jennifer turned left slowly on to the gravel road, the main road into town. But now something was worrying her. She glanced at her sister sitting next to her.

"Steph, I think something's wrong with the truck. The brakes didn't feel right back there."

Stephanie put down her shopping list. She was quiet for a moment thinking. "Go slowly just in case." she said. "There are no more stops or turns until town and the garage is the first on this side. Maybe you better put the emergency blinkers on."

Jennifer shifted down from drive to third gear. For the next five minutes they drove on. Two cars, a faded blue Chrysler and a red Honda, obviously impatient with the truck's slow speed passed leaving dust and stone chips in the air as they went by.

The driver of the faded blue Chrysler glanced quickly at the young woman driving as he sped by. It hadn't taken him long to locate the truck. The young attendant at the only garage around had been quite helpful. It wouldn't be long now. Once the truck was at the garage he would sneak in during the night. The idea had come to him yesterday but the owner needed a good reason to take the truck to the garage and he had provided that reason last night while everyone was busy with guests and a smoking chimney. Why he hadn't thought of the chimney as a diversion himself he didn't know but it was a lucky break for him.

The town was up ahead. The Shell sign was visible and luckily it was on the right-hand side of the road so the truck wouldn't have to stop before turning. Jennifer shifted down to second to help the truck slow down without using the brakes. Their speed was still too fast to pull over and she pulled the lever down to first. There was a large parking area near the garage office and Jennifer turned off the main road then braked. The pedal fell flat to the floor not stopping the truck immediately but slowing it down to a coast as it passed the parking area.

"Use the emergency brake!"

Jennifer had forgotten about this other brake. It worked separate from the main braking system and stopped them in front of the garage bay with a jolt. Jennifer leaned back against the seat and gave a sigh.

"I never want to do that again." she said.

Stephanie sat, stunned for a moment then gave Jennifer a discerning look. "Jen, could you imagine if we had gas tanks in the back and this happened on the road?"

Stephanie got out of the truck slowly and got the attention of the mechanic working on a car in the bay. Jim LaCroix had owned the garage for over ten years and knew everyone around especially those who were dependent upon gas during the summer season. He knew Stephanie and Sam and had written up the safety on their previous vehicle. Stephanie and Jim talked for a moment then Jim walked with her looking over the truck as he came toward Stephanie's side door. Behind the truck near the turn off to the station was a large oil stain on the asphalt.

"Looks like your brake line burst." He looked at Jennifer sitting in the front seat. After a brief introduction he got back to the problem at hand. "Did your pedal go to the floor as you pulled in?"

"Yes, but I felt something was wrong back at the intersection to the lodge."

"Each press of the pedal ejects fluid from the line. You now have no brakes judging from that puddle."

Stephanie looked concerned now. "Jim, do you have time to check it for us now? Sam's alone at the lodge."

Jim wiped his hands with a grey rag tucked in his coveralls. "Well, I'm just finishing up the Ford. The owner won't be in for it until tomorrow morning, so let's take a look."

A young man came out of the office to attend to a customer in a jeep that had pulled up past the pumps.

Jennifer started up the truck and barely touching the gas steered the vehicle into the service bay past the metal lifts and then pulled the emergency brake again.

Outside Stephanie was talking to the owner of the jeep, Mike Kelly. He had seen Sam's truck as he was driving back from town and seeing the emergency lights flashing, decided to stop and see if he could be of help. Jennifer stood next to Jim as he raised the truck up high enough to view the undercarriage. The brake line was dripping the last of the brake fluid. Jim checked the hose then looked at Jennifer. "It's been cut half way through."

"Cut?"

"Your brake line was cut!" echoed a voice behind her. Jennifer turned around and saw Mike Kelly standing at the bay door with her sister.

Jennifer felt a flutter then composed herself. "It looks that way." She remembered the evening before and the sound she had heard behind the office. "Jim, could this have happened last night while the truck was parked?"

"The fluid would only leak as you used the brakes. Yes, someone could have cut the hose then waited for you to drive."

Stephanie and Mike joined them in the bay. Stephanie had that concerned look on her face again. "Jennifer, what are you saying?"

"Last night I heard a sound coming from behind the office. I thought it was some animal so I didn't think much of it, but now I wonder if someone was there."

"That would mean someone's been lurking around the lodge at night?" She saw the look on Stephanie's face then realized now how that must have sounded. But it made sense and could explain the trap incident.

Then trying to diminish the effect she said calmly, "Tyler's cabin is opposite our parking area. We can ask him if he heard anything."

Jim was already getting the replacement part from a shelf along the wall. He looked at the new hose in his hand. Having over heard the girls' conversation he glanced at Mike then said, "You know, I've been working on cars for a long time and to me it looks like it was cut with some small knife." He chose the necessary wrench needed to loosen the damaged hose, "But you can't rule out that it also might have been a defective hose."

Stephanie took a look under the truck. A few drops of fluid escaped landing next to her foot as Jim removed the hose. "Jen, take a look in the truck, would you, and see if you can find a bag or cloth to wrap this in." She passed the dripping hose to Jennifer. Stephanie was focused now on what had to be done. "Will it take long to fix Jim?"

"Maybe half an hour."

Jennifer and Mike examined the broken hose before it went safely away in a garbage bag that Sam kept in the front of the cab. Mike shrugged as if indicating he couldn't be sure whether it was cut or broke apart on its own.

"Would you like a lift back?" offered Mike.

"Thanks Mike, but Stephanie and I will be alright. Besides we have to take gas back to the lodge."

"Well ladies, I leave you in capable hands," he said loud enough for Stephanie to hear. Jennifer walked with him to the jeep. After doing up his seat belt he looked down at Jennifer then over at the garage bay. "You don't believe the hose was defective, do you?"

"No, and I know I heard something last night." He nodded in agreement at her conclusion. "Thank you for stopping, we should be alright now." She looked back at Stephanie by the truck. "Mike, would you do us a favour and let Sam know what's happened and that we shouldn't be too long."

"Sure. Watch yourself driving home. You and the Misha plate seem to attract trouble."

Jennifer watched as he pulled out onto the main road then rejoined her sister in the garage.

Stephanie gave her sister a knowing smile. "He's very nice."

"Yes, he is." Jennifer thought about the time they first met. His strong arms, his gentleness, his steel blue eyes and then there was the duck. She smiled, "I asked him to stop in and let Sam know what happened."

"Sam's got the portable phone," reminded Stephanie. "We could call him from here."

"Oh, does he?" Jennifer gave her sister one of those looks. "I guess I forgot." Then she smiled.

It was midafternoon when the girls finally left LaCroix's garage. They had abandoned the idea of stopping at the craft store and only stayed long enough to pick up the gas, worm boxes and a few groceries. On the return trip Jennifer struggled with Stephanie's idea of sabotage. Even for the short time she had been there she could see now that something wasn't right. "Steph, I didn't tell you about something that happened this morning."

"What do you mean?"

"This morning when I went to get a boat for number five, I couldn't get the motors to start. Sam tried but they wouldn't work, and he had just repaired them the day before." Taking her eyes off the road for a second, she could see that worried look come over Stephanie again. "Now I see what you meant on the phone, this is more than just bad luck." She turned back onto the narrow road heading for the lodge. A faded blue Chrysler staying a good distance behind, continued on down the gravel road past them.

Both were calm now after their initial shake up an hour ago. So, Jennifer decided to confide her thoughts about the hose. "Even though Jim's not absolutely sure, I think the hose was cut, but we'll ask Tyler, he should have been nearby." Meant to lessen Stephanie's reaction she got an unexpected agreement.

"I think so too," said Stephanie.

"You know, something Mike said just now made me think this might be about the truck. He said 'You and the Misha plate seem to attract trouble.' But you've had no problem with it until I started to drive. Maybe it's me."

Stephanie was interested now more than worried, "Then how do you explain the other incidents around the lodge?"

"I don't know, but you and I are going to figure it out," she said determinedly. Stephanie gave her a conspiratorial grin. Then she added softly, "I'm sorry I didn't take your concerns more seriously."

On the return trip the two had discussed whether to report the incident to the Provincial Police, and they decided to wait and see what Sam thought.

Jennifer drove them home and was glad the chore was done. It felt good to be back in the safety of Painted Rock Lodge. Down the lodge road past the car park area, Stephanie noticed Mike Kelly's jeep parked with the other guest vehicles. "Looks like you'll have enough help unloading the tanks." said Stephanie, and she nodded toward the parked jeep. "Funny how he's shown up every time you're driving and something happens."

Jennifer didn't say so but she was glad Mike Kelly had decided to stay. She felt a flutter of excitement.

After dropping Stephanie off at the lodge with the groceries, Jennifer drove on to the boathouse with the tanks of gas then backed the truck in as close as she could to the entrance. Jennifer got out and expected the two men to join her. The light was filtering into the boathouse now from the front entrance. Inside the two men were engaged in conversation and seemed to be working on the motors together. Jennifer could see that the labelled gas tank and two of the boats were gone. The two defective motors had obviously been repaired and assigned and she knew that the Nelson party had arrived safely and Sam had taken care of the registration.

"Well, I'm glad you're back. Mike said you were both okay but I was still a little concerned about your return trip with all that gas in the back. I spoke to Jim about the hose. He said, to him it looked cut but it might also have been a defective hose." Sam came over and put his arm around Jennifer's shoulders and she could feel how tired he was as he leaned over on his good foot. "I'll talk to Stephanie about calling the police."

"I see you fixed the motors." Jennifer gave him an affectionate hug.

"I wouldn't have if Mike hadn't shown up and given me a hand. There was some problem with the spark plugs and the gas line."

"Please don't mention gas." They both laughed.

Jennifer stood in the doorway and found herself staring. She was suddenly aware of how handsome Mike Kelly really was. She watched as he wiped his hands on a rag that was draped over the edge of a wall shelf. There were smudges of grease on his face. He looked like a young boy who had been playing in the dirt with his toy trucks.

"Here, you missed a spot." Jennifer came closer and took the rag from his hand. Those steel blue eyes stared into hers. The thin moustache stretched into a grin. She tried not to let her hand shake.

There, that's a little better." Jennifer tried to smile back but his gaze paralysed her. His hand reached up and touched hers as he took back the worn rag.

"Thanks. It wouldn't do to show up for supper with a dirty face. Sam, I'll help you with those." Mike gave her one more faint smile then left her side to help unload the heavy gas tanks from the truck.

He was staying for supper. Jennifer decided to go back to the lodge and see if Stephanie needed any help.

Chapter 6

The dining room was quiet now, but nearer supper time the couple and brother-in-law from cottage ten and the honeymoon couple would be joining them. She had noticed from the registration card in the office, the new residents from cottage four would be dining out for this evening also.

The window curtains in the dining room were drawn and Jennifer could see Glen and Derek from the side window as they pulled into their previous dock at cottage seven. Derek gave her an enthusiastic wave which Jennifer returned with a nod. She was glad she had moved them back to number seven on her own without their help.

The kitchen area was small and one of the many changes Stephanie had proposed when they first took over the lodge, was to enlarge the room and upgrade the appliances. Stephanie was just spicing up the roast of pork that would be tonight's meal. The roasting pan was large and as always Stephanie would surround the roast with peeled potatoes shortly before the roast was done. Stephanie lowered the oven door. "Let me help you." Jennifer grabbed a towel from the table ready to help her fit the pan into the hot oven.

"It's cold!" Stephanie waved her hand across the bottom element but there was no heat. "It's not working!" She tossed her towel onto the floor missing the table. "Now what do we do?"

Jennifer played with the dial, turning it off and on again. "Wait...look." Jennifer turned on one of the stove burners. "The burners are working, it's just the oven. Could it be a fuse?"

"Maybe, I'll go and check the fuse box."

Stephanie looked nervously at the kitchen clock. There were three hours left until supper time. The girls looked at each other. This was one more little annoying incident. "I know," said Jennifer. "This is a new appliance and shouldn't be having a fuse problem already." Jennifer felt Stephanie's anxiety. After losing your truck brakes and spending wasted time in a garage this was the last thing that needed to go wrong. "I'll see if Sam knows where to look for a fuse."

The kitchen door led out to the steps that joined the path along the beach and to the boathouse. Sam and Mike were unloading the last of the tanks from the truck and both looked up when they heard Jennifer coming. Sam slammed the truck's tailgate up leaving a grimy smudge where his hand had been.

"Sam, could you come and help Stephanie with the stove? The oven won't work."

Sam's look suddenly turned to disbelief, "That's odd, it's a fairly new stove. Stephanie must really be upset. It's getting close to supper time."

Mike was lifting the last of the gas tanks into place in the storage area. "I know a little about wires and fuses, I can go," offered Mike, then walked the same path Jennifer had used back to the kitchen.

"I like your Mike Kelly."

Jennifer locked her arm in his as they walked. "What do you mean my Mike Kelly. He hasn't even made a pass at me. He's probably married or something."

"No, he's not, I asked him."

"You asked him!"

Sam smiled at the panic on Jennifer's face. "Don't worry. We were just chatting. Besides I thought he wasn't your type."

"He's not, but what did he say?" Jennifer slowed their walk up a little so they wouldn't get back to the kitchen before she could find out more from Sam.

"Well, he got back from Europe a few months ago. He was in Croatia and is taking it easy for a few weeks before starting a job in Toronto next month. The jeep is his and the station wagon belongs to a friend who loaned it to him while his jeep was being serviced in Toronto. Anything else, Miss?" Jennifer gave his arm a little hug.

Next to the kitchen door three humming bird feeders hung from a cropped pine tree. Jennifer could hear the buzzing as four maybe five birds whizzed back and forth from the feeder to the surrounding trees. They made a small chirping sound and chased each other around the hanging feeders. Sitting triumphantly, a brightly coloured male perched on one of the curved rungs near a plastic red flower drank his fill and refused to budge as two females hovered in midair above him. Jennifer had never seen one up close before and couldn't imagine how small their babies must be or how they made their nests using such long beaks. Stephanie met them at the door. "The fuse that controls the oven is burned out and we don't have one that will fit." Despite the problem Stephanie seemed relaxed as if everything was under control. "Mike gave me a suggestion. I'll cut the roast up into steaks and we can barbecue them in time for tonight."

"Good." said Sam. "I was starting to think we wouldn't get any supper tonight." He put his arm around

Stephanie. "Now that everything is under control do you mind if I go up and rest for a while?"

Stephanie turned and put her arms around him and gave him a kiss. "We'll call you when supper is ready."

Mike was pushing the stove back into its place in the corner. "Now Miss Stephanie, point me to your barbecue."

Stephanie checked the time on the kitchen clock, a Felix the cat clock, one that Jennifer had given her four years ago when Stephanie had moved out into her own apartment.

"We've got a good hour before lighting up, why don't you two take a break and relax for a while."

"Is there anything that needs to be done first?" asked Jennifer. She didn't want to leave Stephanie alone but she was obviously back in her working mode and seemed fine after a stressful afternoon.

Stephanie was choosing the potatoes she would need for tonight then closed the lid on the bin. "Tyler should be back any minute now. He's not staying for supper but he'll do the garbage run before he goes." She tossed the potatoes into the sink. "The tuck shop can stay closed for the rest of the day, I don't think anyone will come by now, and we can take care of number three tomorrow." She tapped the portable phone Sam had returned to her, "I'll bring the booking folder in here."

Jennifer and Mike left Stephanie to her kitchen and went back out the side door past the humming bird feeder.

It was a beautiful afternoon for canoeing. The water was calm and the sky was clear with just a wisp of cloud in the west. In front of the lodge was a large island that helped to protect the lodge bay from the prevailing winds.

Past this island they could see the guide boat returning with the guests from cottage six. It must have been a good day. The man in the front, probably the father, was waving and holding his arms up as if to indicate the size of the fish they caught.

The two followed the foot path toward the beach and met the boat as it pulled into the docking area for number six cottage. Everyone was excited and Jennifer could see one fish, obviously larger than the 18–24-inch release size, lying across the boat in front of Tyler. Mike helped the older man out and it was clear that he had caught the larger pickerel. "What a fish!" he announced. "You should have seen it!" After retelling the adventure again for Mike and Jennifer's benefit the couple gathered up their rods and retired to their cottage to clean up while her father followed Tyler to the fish cleaning hut to offer his assistance in cleaning the fish. Tyler shook his head slowly. This was one of the few times she saw him smile. Jennifer doubted the father would be much help but Tyler seemed to take it all in his stride.

Jennifer checked the guide boat tank for gas. "There's lots left. How are you with boats?"

"Better than I am with ovens." They put the remainder of the fishing gear into the number six boat. Mike steadied their boat as she got into the middle seat, then gave her the front rope to hold until he started the motor. Jennifer was glad that Tyler had returned in time. If they had taken a canoe ride, she wouldn't be able to sit comfortably facing him. Tyler had taken the spare rod and reel from the boathouse and a small tackle box with the means to help with any line emergency a guest might have. Often a guide would fish along with the others in the group if not enough had been caught for a shore lunch. But today it didn't look as if the rod had been used. It was neatly stored away on special clips along the inside of the boat and the tackle box was in its place under the seat.

Mike had backed the boat out enough to turn around then slowed down before adjusting the handle to forward. They took the left exit from the sheltered bay out into the lake.

The boat she had taken over earlier to cottage five was now tied up in its place. Jennifer wondered if the family of five had enjoyed their picnic and if they had found the spot she had described to the father.

The sound of a large motor interrupted her thoughts and Jennifer could see the boat belonging to Glen Malloy heading out to the right of the lodge. She was glad Mike was with her. Ahead the two chubby children of cottage two were fishing from their dock. They waved enthusiastically as Mike and Jennifer passed. An older couple had rented number one, Stephanie had said, but Jennifer had not yet seen them at the lodge. She wondered if they were the serious fishermen type; the kind who stay out all day and only come in when it gets dark or if the weather gets bad.

Just past cottage one a huge grey rock jutted out into the lake. Its massive sheer face dove straight down into the water. Gentle waves from their boat splashed up against the rock creating a slapping sound. It seemed very deep here and together with the island created a narrows one passed through to reach the major part of the lake.

Jennifer turned to her right to look at the high grey rock. Not visible from the lodge side but clear to anyone approaching, was the reason for the lodge's name. Faded white animals covered the flat face of the rock. No one seemed to know how old they were but the locals Sam had said knew they were ancient Ojibwa pictures. Whether or not that was true didn't really seem to matter. They were beautiful and represented the history of the lake.

Mike followed her gaze and seemed to appreciate the paintings as well. "I haven't been to this side of the lake yet. It's really beautiful and quiet."

"Imagine trying to paint up there." she said. "I wonder what it was like living here thousands of years ago?"

Up ahead was a rock beneath the water that Sam had marked with a plastic bottle. Further up on the left was the bay Jennifer had thought would be a nice place for a picnic. Mike had kept the motor at a nice slow pace and she could see that he was enjoying the beauty of the lake.

Jennifer suddenly caught herself staring at him. She thought about the romance novels she had brought with her but hadn't opened yet. She wondered if "Wilderness Love" had a chapter like this. She suddenly felt awkward and didn't know what to say. His eyes searched the shoreline ahead then focused on her.

"Do you like to fish?" he asked.

"Yes, but I haven't been for a few years."

Mike handed her the rod. "I'll slow the motor so you can troll." He passed her the tackle box as well. Jennifer was glad Sam had an assortment of lures and she chose one that looked interesting. The guide boat hugged the shoreline for a while as Jennifer let out a length of line behind the boat then sat back and relaxed. She could feel the vibration of the lure as it spun below the surface of the water.

"You don't seem to upset about what happened today," observed Mike.

Jennifer switched the rod to her left hand so she could feel the line with her right. "We were a little shaken up. But Stephanie and I don't get easily upset. I'll admit I don't like the idea of someone sneaking around the lodge causing trouble," she repositioned herself on the wooden seat, "but I'm not sure we can do much about that other than be watchful."

Mike slowed the motor down. He was finding it difficult to hear Jennifer with the boat going and seemed to want to talk. They were just in front of the bay now and the boat would drift slowly in towards the large flat rock.

Just as the motor stopped Jennifer felt a hit then a tug. She jerked the rod up then started to reel in. "I've got one!" Mike smiled at her excitement. Then the tugging stopped and the line suddenly felt free. "No, just weeds."

Jennifer reeled in slowly. She would have to pull the weeds off before casting out again. "We thought we'd let Sam decide what to do. I don't know what the police can do, really, other than take the report. After all they didn't do anything after I was forced off the road."

"I enjoyed working with Sam today." Mike hesitated for a moment before speaking as if he wasn't sure he should be talking about Sam's affairs. "Do you know there have been a lot of things going wrong at the lodge?"

"Yes, and I know Stephanie thinks Sam's accident was no accident. That someone planted that trap there. Now the truck seems to be involved somehow."

The lure was jiggling along the top of the water now as Jennifer pulled it toward the boat. She leaned over to grab the line and pull the lure up, so she could reach the weeds easier. Dangling a foot out of the water the lure hung there. "No weeds." Just as she held the line, a fish, larger than the one the father had caught, sprang vertically out of the water having followed the lure back to the boat.

Jennifer screamed and dropped the line. The fish's body slapped the side of the boat next to Jennifer as it fell back into the water abandoning the bait. It was a pike at least three feet long. She had seen its teeth. Mike was standing now reaching for her arm.

"Are you hurt? Did it bite?"

"No. It just frightened me." The rod had fallen in the boat and the lure bobbed awkwardly now on the surface of the lake.

Steadying himself with one hand Mike moved next to Jennifer and put his arm around her. He could feel her trembling. "I thought you don't get frightened easily."

She buried her face in the softness of his shirt and returned the hug. She could hear his heart beating. Her breathing calmed and she felt safe.

Mike stroked her hair. "We better get back, or do you want to fish some more?"

Jennifer smiled and leaned back so she could see his face. Those blue eyes were fixed on her now. His arm still comforted her but his other hand caressed her hair then slid behind her neck gently pulling her toward him. His cheek brushed hers and she could feel his lips near hers. She felt a tremble of another sort.

Then the boat rocked putting them off balance. Derek Kerr whistled and waved as he and Glen Malloy whizzed by them. She wondered what Derek was shouting, then hoped no one else could hear him.

There was a breeze in the air now and the clouds that had been a wisp in the west were now gathering above them. It took a few moments for the rocking of the boat to ease up as the waves caused by Glen Malloy's boat rolled towards the flat protruding rock. Mike returned to his place by the motor. The boat was drifting in backwards now and soon the propeller would be dangerously near the cluster of rocks below the surface. "Maybe we should be heading back," suggested Jennifer.

Mike started the motor on the first pull then pointed their boat back towards the painted rock. They could hear Derek laughing as Glen Malloy headed his boat up the channel. Jennifer was feeling a little awkward now. Had she wanted Mike to kiss her? At that moment probably yes but now after being interrupted like that she felt embarrassed and a little angry that Derek and Glen had seen them and spoiled the moment. Her mood passed quickly as Mike swerved their boat in a meandering pattern which caught them in their own wake rocking the boat gently as it headed home. He gave her a shy smile and she laughed as she pretended to lose her balance with the roll of the hull and grabbed the edge of her seat.

The smell of a barbecue burning off a previous night's remnants met them once they were back in the safety of the bay. Sam was up and had started to get things ready for Stephanie. He waved as they went by. Passing the main dock Jennifer watched as Mike Kelly handled the boat and docked it in its place in the boathouse. Tyler was packing away the worm boxes and stopped to help catch the front of the guide boat as it pulled in. Jennifer had replaced the lure and was just adjusting the rod on its clips as Mike tied the back end to the dock.

Tyler helped her out. "Any bites?"

Jennifer dusted the back of her jeans off. "Boy, do I have a fish story for the guy in number six. You should have seen it, Tyler. It was this big." And she stretched her arms out to their full extent.

Tyler smiled. "I hope you didn't bring it back for me to clean."

"No, and I'm sure it's telling a great story about me right now." The thought of its teeth made her shudder.

"Well, I'm getting hungry," said Mike, "and I promised to do the cooking."

Together Jennifer and Mike walked back to the lodge kitchen. Past the lodge to the left something caught her eye. A man was walking around the trees beyond the beach area, his arms held out and his hand turning, winding something. She hadn't seen him before and supposed it was someone from cottage four. "What's he doing?"

Sam joined them at the side of the lodge and could see they had noticed their newest guest. "He's Mr. Nelson's English visitor. They came back from fishing about ten minutes ago. Nelson thought he'd show off the lake a bit while the ladies unpacked." Sam stopped to set down the brush he was holding so he could use his hands to further tell the story. "When they pulled up to their dock, I could see Mr. Taylor sitting in the middle seat holding this huge mass of matted line. He looked like someone holding a frightened wig." They all laughed. "Apparently he was using his father's favourite reel, a large blue ball contraption." Sam's hands took the shape of the plastic ball. "But once he started to fish the ball popped apart and the line burst out into a tangled mass on his lap. Now he's over there trying to untangle it and wind it back on the reel."

Supper that evening was delicious and the conversation interesting. Mr. Taylor and his sister were visiting Canada for the first time and were thoroughly enjoying their experiences so far. John Taylor sat across from Jennifer at the Nelson table and seemed to find her most intriguing. He was a tall fair-haired man in his early thirties. A police officer stationed in London; he was now here on a three-week vacation. His hair was quite short which gave him that military look. He was a good-looking man and his English accent gave him a further attraction. Jennifer found herself fascinated by his stories. "My last case," he paused, as Stephanie placed a chocolate sponge cake dessert before him, "was ten days ago. Very interesting. A homicide, dating almost twenty-eight years ago. A woman drowned in her swimming pool, only we discovered she had drowned in a swampy area nearby before she was placed in the pool. Her husband was the first suspect, but as it turned out it was the husband's brother and her former lover."

Mike had elected to help Stephanie with the food while Sam entertained the cottagers at a nearby table with hopes of that ultimate catch. Mike had been quiet during most of the meal and seemed to enjoy just watching his new friends interact with their guests.

Stephanie noticed the glances he gave Jennifer. She was sitting across from Mike now that dessert was served and offered him another cup of coffee. "Thank you for helping Sam today," she said, "I know he enjoyed your company."

Mike smiled, "I'm glad I could be of help," then added, "I like Sam, he's easy to get along with."

Stephanie laughed, "I think so too."

Chapter 7

Outside the clouds thickened and covered the blue of the early evening. A slight gust of wind fluttered the leaves into showing their undersides. The badly needed rain had arrived. The rain continued on as a light drizzle until early the next morning. After a quick bite to eat Jennifer started her day by tackling the laundry that was beginning to pile up, then raking the sand in the beach area, ridding it of any debris that was washed up during the night. This was the first time she had noticed the mosquitoes being so bothersome. Returning to her room she decided to change to a shirt with long sleeves and use some of the bug repellent Sam had given her earlier. Across from the dining room area the two chubby children were playing on the main dock. Miniature nets in hand they laughed trying to catch the small minnows that swam in schools around the floating platforms. The morning air was warm and pockets of mist hung over distant areas of the lake. The father of the three young children waved a farewell to his family standing on number five's dock. "Catch a big one Daddy," encouraged one of the twins, as he motored past the main dock area, careful not to create a wake.

Jennifer was eager to finish the floor in number eleven but before that there were humming birds to feed and worm boxes to get ready for the tuck shop fridge. Noon found Jennifer finishing up the bathroom tiles in cottage eleven and ready for a lunch break. She gathered up the numerous papers that had backed the tile and the sticky cut bits that she had trimmed away while fitting the tile around pipes.

There was a noise on the front porch as if someone was coming up the steps. "Hi, who is it?" Jennifer thought it might have been John Taylor stopping by to see her handiwork. She had mentioned finishing up the floor during supper.

"It's me, Derek." Still gathering up the mess she had made Jennifer peered around the hall door. He stood in the doorway in one of those rehearsed poses. "I wondered if you wanted to take a break and go for a ride. I know a quiet little bay not far from here." he grinned.

Jennifer felt her pulse quicken. It was obvious by his look that Derek had the wrong idea about what he had seen yesterday, but she wasn't about to explain it to him. "I've got work to do," she said curtly.

"I'll help you." His hand reached for the door knob intending to close it.

As he stepped in Jennifer could see another man through the screen door. It was Tyler.

"Stephanie and Sam need you at the office," he said matter-of-factly. Derek gave him an annoying look then left.

"Thanks, Tyler. I'm not sure what I would have done if he had persisted." Together they finished cleaning up. Then it occurred to Jennifer that Sam and Stephanie might really be waiting for her at the office.

"No, but I know your lunch will be ready soon," he said. Then he looked at Jennifer, "I saw him head this way so I thought I'd see what he was up to."

Tyler carried the crushed boxes and paper back with them. As they passed cottage seven, Derek turned away from the gas barbecue he was scraping. He picked up a can of beer he had placed momentarily on a fallen log then sat in a wooden chair facing the lake, watching them.

"I'll be glad when he's gone," confessed Jennifer.

Approaching the lodge Tyler stopped and looked at the lake. The cool rain had created a low fog over the water. "My family once lived on this land."

"Your family?"

"Yes, back in the 1930's" He had that expressionless look he had when Jennifer first met him and his eyes seemed to be remembering something he was too young to have known.

"My Great Grandfather's cabin was once here where the lodge now stands," Tyler seemed to come out of his trance like state then gave Jennifer a weak smile, "but that was a long time ago." He readjusted the load he was carrying. "I'll take this to the bins."

Stephanie had prepared a hot lunch for them and the three sat at the office table enjoying one of her cream soup specialties. Tyler had the rest of the day off and decided to go to town before going home.

"Oh, this is good, Stephanie." Cream soups were way beyond Jennifer's talents.

"I hear you've been working on the floor tile in number eleven. How's it going," enquired Sam.

"Fine, I finished up sooner than I expected." The bathroom had been a little tricky but the large removable flanges around the pipes had helped to hide the larger holes needed to fit the tile tightly.

"Good, once we get the furniture back in, we'll have another one ready to rent. What do you think, Steph?"

Stephanie gave her sister an enthusiastic smile. "We have two twin mattresses already. It just means a queen to buy and the wood for the frames." She took another spoonful of soup before continuing, "We have enough furniture and kitchen supplies stored in number twelve," she paused thinking, "maybe in a week or two if you and Tyler can get the beds ready."

The rain had stopped but the leaves were still dripping outside the office screen window. The sound of a motor could be heard off in the distance. The fishermen were starting out again. Jennifer thought of the couple in number one, the painted rock, the pike, ... Mike.

"You look deep in thought," said Sam.

"I was just thinking about the one that got away." Then she smiled hoping Sam hadn't read her mind.

From her place opposite the window, Jennifer could see John Taylor walking toward them from the beach path. He waved as he passed heading to the tuck shop door. Fishing tackle lined two walls of the room. A small refrigerator in the corner held the worm boxes. Shelves on the other side of the room held a variety of snacks and reading material, sun screen lotion and bug repellent. The tuck shop was accessible from the office and John Taylor smiled when he saw Jennifer walk in.

"Good afternoon," he said as he walked over to the tackle wall. "We're going fishing shortly. Do you have any small weights?"

Jennifer checked the adjacent wall and found a package of small round weights. "Are these too small?"

John Taylor went over and checked the package she handed to him. "No, the size is right, but... do you have any that aren't lead?"

Jennifer checked the wall again. Columns of small packages each with their special shape, weight or size hung on small hooks waiting for inspection. "Apparently not, I'm sorry."

"Back home lead has been banned," he explained. "Lead is taking a toll on our wildlife and fish." He looked at the package again as if he was committing a crime. "These will be fine." He smiled and placed the package of weights on the counter. Then as if he had just remembered his main reason for coming in, he said, "I also need four dozen worms."

Jennifer took four boxes out of the refrigerator. She felt John Taylor watching her as she totalled the amount on number four's tab. "Enjoy your day. There are some big ones out there."

Jennifer watched as he went back down the path toward cottage four and a waiting Mr. Nelson in a boat already running and ready to go.

Jennifer hadn't been in the tuck shop before. It was a small room off the office and seemed to be well stocked. She recognized some of the items she had picked up for Stephanie in Sudbury. Next to the counter was a small box used to collect old newspapers. These would be recycled at the lodge for use in the boathouse and during the colder weather, the dining room fireplace.

She glanced at the last contribution; an American paper obviously left by the former occupants of number four. One line, heading a smaller new report jumped out at her 'Death of Renson's Owner-Now Murder.' Jennifer picked up the top folded section and hurried back to show Sam and Stephanie.

Sam was quiet for a few moments after reading the article. "It's the same garage. It seems he died sometime in February when he was crushed by a raised engine he was working on." paraphrased Sam. "It was discovered recently by the new owner, his nephew, that the place had been robbed earlier. Many of the February receipts were missing. The theft prompted further investigation and they now know that the death was no accident. They're looking for a former associate of his who got out of prison a few days before the murder."

Jennifer and Stephanie had both been silent during this revelation.

"It's too bad," said Sam, "he seemed like a nice guy."

"Well, I guess that explains the Visa bill." Stephanie started to clear away the dirty dishes, while Jennifer spooned up the last of her soup.

A vehicle coming up the road distracted her from imagining all kinds of reasons for Renson's death. Mike Kelly pulled up in the small parking space next to Jennifer's Mustang. He waved when he saw them through the office screen. Sam greeted him at the door and offered him a cup of coffee. "I was in town so I picked up a couple of fuses for you." He traded Stephanie the cup of coffee for the fuses in his hand. "I couldn't bear the thought of barbecuing in the rain."

"Thanks Mike, that was kind of you," said Stephanie. Mike sat quietly next to Sam and sipped on his coffee while the girls cleared off the last of the dishes. Sam smiled secretly to Stephanie then broke the silence.

"The motors we fixed are running well, thanks to your help."

"Anytime, Sam. Actually, it gets a little boring over there at times and I welcomed the change."

Jennifer had joined them again and sat opposite Sam. "You mean wrestling ducks doesn't fill your day." Then she laughed tossing her dark hair back with one hand.

Mike smiled remembering how silly he must have looked. "I believe you have a rain check for supper, Miss Jennifer." He used Sam's expression to avoid feeling formal.

"Yes, and I do believe it rained today," she added keeping the conversation light.

"I'll meet you at the dock by six?" He smiled at Jennifer's nod then left explaining he had an errand.

Sam was quiet until the jeep was well down the drive. "Is that a date, Miss Jennifer?"

"Is what a date?" asked Stephanie. She had caught the tail end of the conversation and noticed Sam grinning.

"No, it's just supper. And just so you know, I was planning to wash my hair this afternoon anyway."

By five o'clock Jennifer was sitting on the main dock, enjoying the afternoon sun and letting her hair dry in its warmth. There was a glow and a silvery shimmer to the trees she hadn't noticed before and the reflected light danced along the shore line flickering as the breeze caught the leaves. With the return of the sun, mosquitoes took refuge in the undergrowth but would probably be buzzing in full force again by dusk.

The lake was calm and quiet except for the droning sound of a boat returning to the lodge. It was Mr. Nelson and his English fishing buddy. Mr. Nelson pulled up to the main dock very slowly and shook his head in a manner that suggested he couldn't do too much about his guests fishing ability. Jennifer took the front rope then saw the source of Mr. Nelson's frustration. In John Taylor's lap was a frazzled ball of line.

Jennifer smiled at the tangled mess. "Well, I see you've been fishing."

"Yes, and I had one on the line," he added proudly. "What a great day!" John Taylor was grinning ear to ear. Jennifer held the boat steady as he stepped out clutching the line so it wouldn't drag on the dock. "I should untangle this straight away so we can fish again after supper," he added.

Mr. Nelson just smiled. He was glad that John was the patient type and not easily put off by little setbacks. "I'll leave the gear in the boat then," he decided, "the worms should be alright in the cooler. Don't be long."

The ladies from number four waved a greeting from their deck. They had taken the opportunity to sit out and sunbathe while the men were fishing.

Jennifer and John Taylor watched as Mr. Nelson made his way up the rock path to their cottage. "Would you like some help with your line?"

"Yes, thank you. I know Jeffrey would rather I try one of his rods but father was so enthusiastic about me taking his that I want to give it a fair chance. He's had the set since '62." He looked puzzled at the line in his hand. "Maybe I'm doing something wrong."

"I doubt that," Jennifer said reassuringly. "Let's use the chairs, the trees are bound to be mosquito territory."

John Taylor handed her the blue plastic globe that housed the reel while he carefully cushioned the ball of line in his two hands. During the twenty minutes it took to unwind the line and string it around two chairs Jennifer got to know a little more about Mr. Nelson's English visitor.

John Taylor was born in London, raised in Bromley Kent and joined the force at the age of nineteen. He was 32 years old and came from a police family, he being the fourth generation, although forensics was a new branch added to the tradition. Jennifer listened eagerly to the details of some of his cases. She could tell that he loved his work.

Once untangled John Taylor began to rewind the line onto the reel while Jennifer kept the line taut and straight.

"The closest I've ever come to anything exciting like that was Friday when someone tried to force me off the road." Jennifer described the details to a very interested listener, and then added the adventure yesterday while picking up the gas for the lodge.

He stopped winding the line and his face took on a concerned puzzled look. "That all sounds a little too coincidental." His blue eyes fixed their gaze on the truck parked beside the office. "And each time you were in the truck?"

"Yes," replied Jennifer, not sure what he was getting at.

"Did you have any difficulty arriving here?" He sounded like a police officer now and Jennifer could see him taking mental notes.

"No. In fact, other than a bumper scrape in a parking lot two years ago, my driving career had been quite uneventful. The mechanic did admit though it could have been a faulty hose."

John Taylor wound the last of the line slowly, careful to secure the end and keep it taut. "Well, that didn't take long." He smiled at their accomplishment. "Thank you again for your help and the pleasant company." Jennifer was close to him now having followed along like a fish caught on the end of his line.

She looked at the line neatly wound back in place. "Now it's my turn to play detective." She made a throat clearing sound before continuing. "Mr. Taylor, have you recently replaced your father's original line?"

John gave her an inquisitive smile, his blue eyes twinkling, and he looked at the enameled reel in his hand. "Why yes, Jeffrey gave me a new spool of line before we arrived here."

"Well, my dear Watson, we have a mystery solved. You, Sir, have too much line on your reel, either because of the amount on our spools or a heavier weight you were given. Not much mind you, but enough to slide off the edge and cause the rest to tangle."

John Taylor shook his head slowly, "I should have thought of that."

Jennifer swatted a mosquito away from her face. "Maybe, but you've never been fishing before so how would you know about fishing line."

He studied the blue globe in his hands and then smiled, "True, but I do know about cut hoses. Too bad it's been repaired already. You've got me interested now."

"Oh, we kept the old one, just in case Sam wanted to report it to the police. It's in the office."

John's sister Louisa was on the deck of their cottage now and upon catching his eye gave him a wave indicating supper was ready.

"Thank you again for your help." Something caught his attention. John Taylor's glance past her indicated company had arrived. "It looks as if we both have to go." Behind her Mike was sitting in his canoe at the dock patiently waiting as the line winding ceremony came to an end. Jennifer said good night and walked toward the dock as John Taylor made his way up to his cottage blue globe in one hand and swatting mosquitoes with the other.

Chapter 8

He wore a green plaid shirt with its long sleeves rolled up his forearm, faded blue jeans and runners. With the sun at his back, sunglasses now adorned his loosely hung hair, his eyes intense upon her. A canoe paddle sat across the top of the canoe as Mike sat back in his seat one arm leaning over the oar. There was a slight smile spreading across his face. "Don't tell me. Mr. Taylor's been fishing."

Jennifer accepted his hand as she stepped into the canoe wondering if he had been waiting long by the dock, then took a seat across from Mike. "Yes, and we've fixed the line problem so you can stop grinning. Besides, I like him."

His face warmed. "So do I." Mike gave the dock a shove and backed the canoe away before starting to guide it in the direction of the boathouse.

At six o'clock the sun was still warm and bright. Ripples of glaring light danced across the water as the canoe glided slowly along the Painted Rock Lodge shoreline. Jennifer glanced at each cottage as they passed and wondered what the occupants were doing. All was quiet. Everyone seemed to be enjoying the last part of the day out on the lake. She was especially glad the boat at number seven's dock was out. Only the honeymoon couple's boat was in its place and she could see the two of them outside at a picnic table enjoying their meal together. Mike caught her gaze and she smiled remembering the earlier incident with the worm bath.

She suddenly caught herself staring at him. His arms, as he manoeuvred the canoe silently along the jagged shore. She could feel herself redden and hoped he hadn't noticed. Then she suddenly thought of something Stephanie had said earlier, about Mike being at each scene of trouble with the truck. She looked at him as he paddled the canoe and smiled to herself. It was a coincidence she decided, a lucky coincidence.

Jennifer focused once again upon the shoreline as they passed the last of the Painted Rock cottages. Number eleven with its new floor was almost ready for new guests but the final cottage needed far more than that. Its exterior was in rough shape as well and it seemed to Jennifer that this must be one of the oldest of the buildings on the lake. They passed along the shore in silence enjoying the quiet. The sudden sound of wild rice flattening against the canoe shell told her they were almost at the beach where Mike had earlier saved so many lives. She smiled remembering how he had looked clutching the wild duck in one hand and fumbling with pliers in the other. She chuckled at the thought.

Mike broke her meditation and lifted his paddle out of the water allowing the canoe to rest on its bed of rice. He pointed to the front section of the repaired dock. "They spend a great deal of time along this shore and often sit together at the far end." He leaned forward as he spoke making it easier to see under the dock. "There's a piece of log sticking up out of the water just there," he pointed, "and sometimes they all scramble up and huddle there together." The underside of the dock was dark with shadow and the sun was in her eyes but it appeared to her that the duck family must be out and about the lake somewhere else. Seeing her disappointment he added, "They usually come around near sunset."

The canoe was in a foot and a half of water now so Mike gave it one last push of the paddle along the sandy bottom and glided it just short of the beach. Seeing she was about to get out Mike steadied the canoe then motioned for her to stay seated. "No reason for us both to get wet." He first removed his runners leaving his feet bare then stepped into the rice field and pulled the canoe up the last few yards on to the sandy beach. Once on solid land Mike reached out his hand for her. "Miss Jennifer?"

"Thank you, Sir." Once out, Mike pulled the canoe further to one side of the sandy beach. A large log, obviously a seating area, provided as tie up. A large ring had been hammered into the end which made fastening the rope secured at the front of the canoe easier. For some reason Mike preferred this to tying up at the newly repaired dock.

Jennifer observed the preparation for supper. On the beach just past the damp edge of the lake where the waves slowly meandered in and out, Mike had set up their dining area. A fire pit, encircled with darkened angular stones took up the centre of the small beach area in front of the log cabin. Two folding chairs stood at one side of the pit and a blanket covered log at the other. Between the log and the two chairs Mike had constructed a make shift table of left-over wooden planks and large rocks. A small arrangement of wild flowers in a plain cottage glass sat in the centre of the table, surrounded by mismatched plates and cutlery one typically found in cottages. At the rear of the table a small cooler hugged the little shade that was offered it. To the left the large stone outcrop, as if waiting patiently for supper, supported an old round barbecue, the kind she and her family had used years ago but this one was minus its legs. A large round piece of metal tubing sat up in the centre.

Jennifer could see that newspaper had been stuffed inside then charcoal poured in up to the top. Mike had been watching her silently up to now delighting in her expression of approval. "This is unusual," she commented.

He was hoping she had noticed the cooking device and never tired of explaining how the chimney pipe method of building a fire worked. "It's something I learned in Europe." He had Jennifer's full attention now. "Look," and he pointed to the cut away sections in the bottom rim of the cylinder, "anything will work actually, even a real stove pipe but you have to cut away little pieces out of the bottom edge first to allow the air to get in."

Jennifer looked away from the marvelous invention to focus on Mike as he explained further. There it was again, that boyish enthusiasm. There was a sparkle in those steel blue eyes. "Then," he went on, "you place crumpled up newspaper inside pushing it to the bottom. Then load up the rest of the tube with charcoal or wood." He fumbled for a moment trying to retrieve matches from his jeans pocket. Once secured he continued his demonstration. "I didn't light it earlier because I didn't like leaving a fire unattended, but it shouldn't take long." He leaned over and struck a match close to the base of the tube. "You light it at the bottom and the paper catches fire." He paused for a moment waiting for the fire to take its cue. "Air coming in from the bottom gives it that chimney effect and in a short time we slowly raise the tube adding more charcoal on top until it's glowing hot."

Jennifer looked on in awe of the whole procedure. "So, you don't need lighter fluid or smelly fuel bricks." She studied the device as the paper quickly caught fire then spread to the charcoal. "This is wonderful! You'll have to share this idea with Sam."

His demonstration a success, Mike let the fire burn and escorted Jennifer to one of the seating areas. "A drink, Miss Jennifer?"

Miss Jennifer. She could tell that Mike was feeling a little awkward and suddenly not at ease.

"Thank you, yes, but call me Jen if you like."

"Okay, Jen." She liked the way his voice softened when he said her name. She smiled up at him from her seat on the blanketed log. Her gaze met his for a moment. A trace of a smile appeared behind that slim moustache then he turned momentarily to fetch her a glass from the table behind him.

"Well," pretending to fold a towel over his left arm, he went on, "we have for supper tonight, Milady, steak cooked to perfection over an open fire, baked potato, Caesar salad and sautéed mushrooms." Jennifer giggled softly as Mike attempted an accent, she wasn't sure belonged to any country. "My name is Mike and I will be your waiter." Not being able to carry on the impression with a straight face any further, Mike laughed.

"That's my friend Ivan. We met in Ljubljana. I've got his accent down pretty good but he always seemed a lot smoother sounding when he spoke English. The ladies liked it."

At the makeshift bar Mike now offered an assortment of beverages before beginning supper. "White wine will be fine, thank you." responded Jennifer and she giggled again softly. "Sam mentioned you had just come back from Europe.

"Yes, and I start work again in September. At home this time. It'll be my first assignment away from conflict. It's made my mother happy."

"What did you do in Europe?"

Mike poured himself a glass of wine then paused to check on the fire before answering. He gave the metal tube a shake and raised it a little. Red coals appeared along the base so he added more charcoal to the top then returned to sit next to Jennifer. "I'm a photographer and I took pictures in the former Yugoslavia. Pictures of the people, the land, the aftermath of war," he paused, his voice saddened a little, "the waste of it all."

Mike adjusted his position and straddled the log seat so he could face Jennifer. "Before I started, I got to stay in Slovenia for two weeks. That's where I met Ivan." His face brightened again. "He was on leave and hooking up with me for a while was better than hanging around the local pubs. Besides, Ivan said it would help him with his English." He paused to take a sip of wine then continued. "The war was virtually over in that province and travelling with one of its soldiers seemed a safe way to see some of the country." His eyes suddenly regained a youthful enthusiasm. "Do you know that I actually met a Bulgarian terrorist?"

Jennifer tilted her head in disbelief. "Really? And how did you know he was from Bulgaria?" Jennifer raised her left leg up resting it on the blanket so she could face Mike better.

Mike waited for her to get comfortable before he started. "We were in Bled. There I was with my camera

93

ready to take a perfectly lit picture of the island in the lake. Ivan had gone to one of the local inns to check on a room for the night." He waited for her while she took another sip of wine before going on with his adventure. A young man also looking at the island asked me in English if I would take a picture of him. He handed me a small Instamatic camera and proceeded to tell me that he was from the States. He was actually born in Bulgaria but could not return there because he'd avoided their compulsory army duty. He said it was nice to speak English to someone again. All the while he was talking, I was aiming the camera at him with the lake in the background."

"But, and here's the interesting part. There was no film in the camera and I seriously doubt if it even worked. So, I went through the motions and clicked the button." Mike set his glass down and once again got up to check on the barbecue. Jennifer followed him with her eyes knowing there must be more to this story. She gave him a look.

"Fire's almost ready." He looked pleased with himself both for his skill in fire making and storytelling. Mike could see Jennifer was resisting the impulse to ask questions. "Oh yes, anyway, just as Ivan rejoined me a black four-door sedan came whizzing up a side street and stopped just long enough for our Bulgarian friend to hop in the back seat. There were three other men in the car and they drove off down the main street out of town. The next day we heard on the radio there had been a bombing in the area by Bulgarian terrorists."

The early hours of evening continued with stories and wonderful food. Jennifer was surprised at how well he prepared the meal. He had declined her offer of assistance and seemed well adapted to the kitchen such as it was. Mike had some of his photos with him and shared them with her. Each one had a story to go with it. She loved his enthusiasm and sensitivity. A second bottle of wine was now opened as the sun gave one last flare before descending to the other side of the world. Once the supper fire was no longer needed Mike transferred the hot coals to the central fire pit then added some small cut up branches. "This should keep the mosquitoes away and the chill off." The blanketed log now was moved back away from the fire pit. A second larger blanket draped over its edge and on to the sandy beach. The log was now a back rest for the two as they sat next to each other gazing at the flames.

"Thank you for a wonderful meal. Stephanie couldn't have done better." Jennifer sighed and stretched her arms out in front of her.

Mike poured them each another glass of wine. "You're very welcome." he hesitated for a moment then added, "I'm glad it rained."

The moon, three quarters full, had just appeared above the cabin bathing the lake before them in sparkling light. The stars shone. More than Jennifer had ever noticed before. "This is a beautiful spot," she said. Jennifer felt Mike's arm around her shoulders now and snuggled closer to him. With the night came a cool damp breath of air.

"I like it, more now," and he gave her a gentle hug. "The cabin's not in the best of shape but it'll do. Apparently, it was built in the '30's, out of logs from this very spot I should think." The fire needed another log and a little stoking. Sparks loomed up then dissipated as they met the moist air. "My friend Tony's mother has owned the property for several years but has never been up here. I suppose the locals would know more of its history."

Jennifer watched the flames as they licked at the new arrivals. "I bet Tyler would know. He said his people once lived on this part of the lake."

Momentary cloud cover blocked the ray of the moon. The stars shone brighter. The forest framed the lake and a loon gave its haunting call. To their left near the tied-up canoe Jennifer heard a rustle in the underbrush. Two small eyes glared at them. Mike felt her tense up. "What is it!"

"Look! Over there!" she whispered. "Two small eyes looking at us."

"It's probably a raccoon thinking he'd get a bit of our leftovers." Then he laughed softly. "Those are two small eyes close together. Now if they were big eyes far apart, I think I would worry more."

"Very funny," Jennifer resumed her relaxed state and snuggled back against his arm. The whining sound of two fishing boats filled the lake and Jennifer could tell they were putting into their respective docks at the lodge. It was that time. She wondered if Sam was waiting up for her as well as the boats. Her eyes wandered further to the left then back to the canoe. The two small eyes had disappeared back into the forest. Mike leaned a little closer to her cheek. He could smell the scent of almonds in her long brown hair and the fragrance coaxed him on.

Jennifer focused back to the left again then gently nudged Mike in the ribs. Then as if she felt the need to whisper, she said, "What about one eye?" Mike followed her gaze. To the left, past the trees that rimmed the beach area a single light was visible.

Mike sat up away from his resting place and unnecessarily stoked the fire again. "That's some sort of light." It flickered, disappeared, then reappeared. He sat back and his arm squeezed around her. He whispered, "Try to relax. If we can see it, it or he can see us."

Jennifer tried to stay calm and not look in the direction of the light. She thought of Derek and their last encounter on the lake. "Is someone spying on us?"

"I don't think so. Wait until I hug you, then try to get a better look." His left arm now reached across her and together both Mike's arms embraced her. Jennifer was able to look past his shoulder and strained her eyes to get a better look at the flickering light. "I didn't know Sam's last cottage was so close," she whispered.

His cheek brushed against hers. "There's not much we can do about it now."

Jennifer leaned away in protest. "Can't we take the canoe and go over ..." His lips found hers and she was suddenly unaware of anything in the universe but Mike. His arms, his lips totally engulfed her.

Chapter 9

She had arrived home just as the last boat docked under the watchful eyes of Sam and Stephanie. It was almost midnight before she finished her story of the mysterious light. Mike had joined them for the recounting and at Stephanie's occasional gaze gave a sheepish grin.

The brake line hose which had been the topic of conversation earlier that evening sat in the centre of a dining room table.

"Mr. Taylor stopped by the office before going out to fish again." Sam raised the hose up then sat it back down as if to emphasize the results. "He said, it's been cut."

Jennifer gazed at Mike, then Stephanie, and then back to Sam. "What do we do now? Call the police?"

Sam smiled then leaned back in his chair as Stephanie handed him a mug of coffee.

"Yes, my young detective." He paused to take a sip then gave Mike a knowing glance. "It's too bad you missed him. Quite nice actually. He did ask to speak to you but Stephanie was able to give him all the details."

Stephanie interjected, her turn to tease, "Tall, sandy-blonde hair, very professional, just your type."

Jennifer gave her long hair a push back then gave Stephanie a look. "Okay, that's enough," she protested, "but, then again, maybe we should call him back to report the light."

Mike, sitting back with his warm mug of coffee in his hands, was content to watch and listen to his friends, enjoying the banter. He had said little after tying up at the dock and escorting Jennifer to the office, but now he added his opinion to the conversation.

"The light looked like a small flashlight. It seemed to flicker on and off because of all the thin trees between it and us. Once we left the beach area it was off," he paused, "but that doesn't mean he wasn't still there watching."

"Watching what?" asked Sam.

"This place, for some reason. Face it, along with the two truck incidents you have had more than your share of bad luck lately."

With these last words Jennifer nodded to Stephanie, agreeing that her sister's initial fears were well founded.

He concluded, "And I don't think it's coincidental." Mike had summed up what each of them was thinking.

Jennifer felt herself shudder. "You think someone is hanging about the lodge watching us, waiting for the chance to cause problems or accidents."

"It makes sense now," said Sam.

"What if we all go over now!" suggested Jennifer. "Sam, you have a rifle. We can ..."

"Whoa, just a minute there Nancy Drew." Sam had resisted the same urge earlier upon hearing of the intruder. "I don't think we're in any danger now. Whoever it is, doesn't know we suspect anything and there've been many opportunities to rob us if that's their goal."

"Sam's right," agreed Mike. "Trying to apprehend him may only cause an unpleasant confrontation and we don't know if he's armed." He placed his empty mug on the table as if preparing to leave. He smiled at Jennifer's frustration and gave her hand a warm squeeze as he got up. "Besides, he or they are trying hard to stay undetected so let's let it stay that way for now."

Sam looked in the direction of number twelve. The dining room drapes were drawn back but the windows had been shut upon Jen and Mike's news. Confident no one could hear their low voices he added, "And before we call the police back, we need something more substantial, some proof."

Jennifer could see Stephanie was upset by the conversation and Sam tried to ease her fears. He got up and gave her shoulders a hug then addressed the other two. "Look, let's keep our eyes open and watch for anything that seems unusual. Everything has to seem normal. We need to catch our culprit red-handed. Mike, are you up for some detective work at number twelve tomorrow?"

"I thought you'd never ask. I'll be over early."

For the remainder of the night, sleep was as elusive as their mysterious stranger. Jennifer kept replaying the evenings events over and over in her mind. Why would someone cause trouble for Stephanie and Sam? Were all the mishaps deliberate and what about the trouble she had had with Sam's truck? Her thoughts drifted back to Stephanie's comment about Mike. If Mike was involved then he had to have an accomplice. No that didn't make sense. She wasn't thinking rationally. The night was playing tricks on her mind now. An owl hooted ceremoniously outside her window. But why were Sam and Mike so calm about a possible intruder especially when there were others at the lodge who might be injured. She thought about the two chubby children and Mr. Tokar and his young children. Maybe she was just over reacting. What if the accidents were just accidents after all and the person spying on them was a guest at the lodge. Maybe it was Derek all along. How long had he been watching them? Sam was right. They needed something more substantial before involving the police.

Jennifer's thoughts wandered back to Mike again. It had been a wonderful evening. She trembled remembering the first time he held her hand. How she fit perfectly in his arms and how they connected on a deeper level. He was someone she felt comfortable with. Someone she could care about. She smiled to herself-yes, someone she could care about.

Raindrops hit the roof of her room sporadically as a low rumbling echoed across the lake, then in a rhythmic beat reminding her of summers past and other cottage vacations. Lightening flashed. "One, one thousand, two, one thousand, three, one thousand, four, one thousand," she counted in a whisper waiting for the next rumble. The storm was about four miles away now.

Jennifer leaned back to get a better look at her bedroom clock, 4:38. Tomorrow would be a busy day. She really had to stop thinking and get some sleep. The rumbling had faded now leaving the drops on wet leaves to gather and fall heavily on the roof above her. An owl hooted again outside her window. Probably the same owl that greeted her that first evening. Wait a minute. The same owl that hooted when she heard the noise behind the lodge. She didn't know much about owls. When do owls hoot? Is it because someone has disturbed them or did, they just call to other owls from time to time. Jennifer tried not to over think the nocturnal habits of an owl. It was late and she was tired. She adjusted her head again on the pillow. What if someone was there right now, just outside the lodge. She had to find out.

The laundry room was accessible from the dining room hallway as was her room and the office. Being closer to Sam's truck it would give a better view.

Reaching for her housecoat Jennifer wiggled her feet into her moccasins. She wouldn't take a flashlight; she was familiar enough with the inside of the room and figured she could get to the laundry room window without being heard. She walked slowly trying not to bump into anything or make noise with her feet as she felt her way along the walls into the small room. It was dark and with the slow passing of the heavy storm clouds across an otherwise beautiful moon she could see nothing but blackness surrounding Sam's truck. Jennifer waited in anticipation of hearing a human sound. Nothing. She waited, then decided this was silly.

Jennifer woke to the sound of a car pulling up beside her bedroom window. As he had promised, Mike was here early.

There was a grey blanket over the lake by the time Jennifer was up and dressed. She had had only two hours sleep but somehow, she didn't feel tired. The day had the promise of excitement and other than help Stephanie with lunch and supper there wasn't a lot that had to be done. Tyler would take care of the garbage and there were no cottages that needed to be readied until tomorrow.

Stephanie was alone in the dining room as she joined her sister for breakfast. Stephanie was sitting quietly at a table for four near the kitchen entrance. She had been going over some book work as Jennifer came in and greeted her with a tired smile. "Have some, I just made it." Jennifer picked up a piece of crispy bacon from a large plate in the centre of the table. Fingers of buttered toast sat around the edge of the plate. "The guys just left to check out number twelve."

Jennifer made herself a mini bacon sandwich then poured herself a cup of coffee from the coffee maker situated on a long sideboard near the kitchen door then offered Stephanie a refill. "Well, I spent half the night thinking about it," confessed Jennifer.

"Really," grinned Stephanie, "I would have thought you had other subjects on your mind."

Jennifer smiled back and deliberately didn't respond as she picked up a second piece of bacon. "I wonder if they found anything? I'll go over and meet them," she gave Stephanie a hopeful look, "unless you need help with breakfast."

"No, go ahead. There's just the couple from cottage six and her father this morning."

Jennifer left the dining room by the side door facing the boathouse. Humming birds flitted from feeders to trees and back again creating a tiny whirling sound as they hovered then chased one another. It was beautiful this time of the morning. The lake was calm and motionless. The grey sky above and the swirling mist drifting above the water gave the lake a mystic primeval look. It was a little chilly this early in the morning and Jennifer was glad she wore a long-sleeved shirt. She could see the men in number eight untie their boat and prepare to leave their dock.

The sound of a motor boat echoed behind her from the other end of camp and she wondered if it belonged to the couple in cottage one. Two of the ladies in number eight stepped out onto their porch to give the men an encouraging send off. Dressed in robes, one clutched a small pink blanket around her shoulders, they gave their husbands a wave then as soon as the motor revved forming a billow of smoke behind the boat, they quickly headed back to the warmth of the cottage.

A noise from the main dock caught her attention. Mr. Nelson was down at his boat. He had his old metal tackle box open on the seat before him, the kind that folded out with three drawers, the kind that often fell over like her father had.

The squeak of a wooden door drew her gaze to the cottage on the hill above Mr. Nelson. John Taylor was making his way down the stairs ready for another excursion into Canadian waters. He was well armed. A large telescopic net rested over one shoulder and his blue bulbous reel and rod were clutched in his right hand along with a small white cooler. The rod was quite long and when not spearing small shrubs along the way as he manoeuvred down the path, bobbed gently at the tip.

He was protected from the elements by a bright yellow rubberized rain coat and pants. A floppy yellow hat completed the ensemble. Mr. Nelson was still looking for something in his tackle box. He appeared to be retying his line and didn't seem in a great hurry to get started.

Jennifer walked along the front of the dining room past the wall of windows. John Taylor smiled broadly upon seeing Jennifer and set his things in the boat before joining her on the sandy beach. "What a wonderful day!" he announced. He swatted his exposed hand, "Well except for the mosquitoes." A loon's call echoed hauntingly beyond the mist. "And listen to that, how beautiful."

His enthusiasm made Jennifer smile. She hoped he had some success in fishing today. Something he could remember for years to come. "Thank you for stopping by the office last night. Sam said your opinion was very helpful, though I don't know if there's much they can do with the report we made."

"You'd be surprised what clues can come together. Sometimes little things can complete the puzzle."

Jennifer glanced over at the boat. Mr. Nelson was still working on his line and didn't seem to be waiting for his guest so Jennifer continued. In a quieter tone so no one else could hear she told John about the flickering light in the last cottage and how she suspected someone had been watching.

"That is curious. I wonder ..." The sound of the motor starting stifled his thought and he turned and gave Mr. Nelson a wave of acknowledgment. "Well, I'd best be off."

Jennifer walked him to the dock. She wondered if the yellow rainwear also belonged to his father. Jennifer steadied the boat as John stepped in and sat in the centre seat facing the front. "See you at lunch," he said.

"Good luck!" Jennifer watched as their boat cut out a path through the mist. It swirled alongside the boat then crowded in around them covering their path behind as they went. Another boat cruised past Jennifer and cut across the narrow channel. Its driver waved and shouted a good morning. Derek Kerr. Jennifer resisted a wave and just smiled politely. It had come from number seven and having picked up more speed than it should have, now cut its power back and fell into line behind Mr. Nelson's boat causing a wake to rock the main dock and slap noisily at the water under it. Jennifer steadied herself on the moving dock and decided to catch up with Mike and Sam. They'd been a while and must have discovered something.

Crossing back in front of the dining room again Jennifer could see Stephanie sitting at the table. She had obviously been watching the show outside her window and gave Jennifer a finger wave as she walked by. Other than the fishermen everyone else seemed to still be in bed. It was early yet and the cloud cover gave the illusion of darkness. A good morning to sleep in.

A humming bird flitted by Jennifer's ear as she invaded the feeder territory again. The boathouse was in darkness but she could see Tyler at the entrance working at the tool bench. "Hi, Tyler," she called. She was eager to tell him about the evening's events. He moved away from the entrance and before Jennifer could call again, he was out of sight.

From the entrance view the boathouse was dimly lit. Light reflecting from the water entrance outlined two boats tied at the dock. Jennifer scanned the interior but no sign of Tyler. She checked outside again and along the beach but he had gone.

"Good morning, early bird." It was Sam and Mike returning from their investigation. Sam greeted her with a warm hug. "I didn't expect to find you out and about yet."

"What and miss all the excitement?" Her eyes had met Mike's as soon as she had turned around from the boathouse entrance and now, they both stood in an awkward silence.

"Well," said Sam, "this is all very nice and I wish I could stay and watch you two look at each other but I have to share this news with Stephanie." Mike smiled warmly seeing Jennifer's embarrassment at Sam's comment.

Jennifer suddenly remembered the purpose for the morning expedition. "You mean you found something?"

"Just these." Mike held out his hand for her to see. On a leaf which he unfolded carefully, sat three cigarette butts and four spent matches. "From where we found these it appears that there was only one person in the cottage last night. And," before Jennifer could comment, Mike added, "these are American cigarettes. I know the brand and you can't buy them here."

Each leftover filter had a tiny ring of print around it indicating the brand.

Jennifer started to get excited then realized she might be overheard. "So, let's say our intruder is an American or someone who has been across the border and prefers this brand. Maybe it's one of the guests!"

"Maybe, but why would one of the guests hang out in a dark empty cottage?"

Jennifer could think of one guest who would probably enjoy spending the night in an empty cottage if it meant he could spy on her but she was uneasy about suggesting Derek Kerr. Instead, she asked, "Is Sam going to ask Stephanie about the guests?"

"Yes, not that it will mean much." Together they followed Sam back to the dining room. They walked in silence then Mike stopped and grabbed her hand in his before she could walk further. Her dark hair tossed as she turned abruptly to face him. Mike smiled, "You know, you are very beautiful this morning, Miss Jennifer." His voice softened as he said her name.

Jennifer glanced away then back at him again. "Why thank you, sir. It did take a bit of doing. Late night, two hours sleep, rainy humid morning." A mosquito buzzed

107

near her ear and she swatted it away distracted for a moment.

He pulled her gently to him. "Jen, thank you for last night. It's been a long time since I've enjoyed such an evening." His face was close to hers.

She wanted to kiss him. To be lost in his arms again. To…

Chapter 10

A tapping sound drew their attention to the dining room window. Sam was waving them in. With his right arm around her shoulder Mike escorted Jennifer toward the lodge. "Come on, let's see what he's found out," he said.

The smell of bacon cooking on the stove greeted them as they entered the dining room door. There were no guests joining them this early so Stephanie had started their own breakfast. Sam was standing next to the sideboard fixing himself a cup of coffee now. Jennifer noticed that he was walking better today and the cane which had been a constant companion since she arrived was absent.

"Two more for breakfast Steph," he announced sitting down next to Stephanie's booking binder. He flipped two pages over indicating their search. "Only two American entries this week. Both couples. Our lovebirds and the reclusive couple in number one. We had a Buffalo family here last week. They left Saturday morning. But that's all."

Jennifer sat next to Sam. She stared at the binder lost in thought. Mike had gone into the kitchen to help Stephanie bring out their plates each laden with a serving of scrambled eggs and bacon strips.

"Thanks, Mike." Stephanie set a plate down for Sam then sat hers beside the closed binder.

"Here, Jen." Mike handed his extra plate to Jennifer then sat in the empty chair opposite Sam.

Sam filled Stephanie in on their hunt. "Well, I'm not sure we have anything worth bothering the police about but let's keep our evidence just in case we need it later."

Mike stood up to show Stephanie the leaf package and unwrapped it carefully while Sam went to a drawer in the sideboard and retrieved a small plastic storage container. As Mike deposited his find for safe keeping the front door of the dining room opened and Mr. Newlywed walked in.

He glanced around at the breakfast table and as if a soft voice would lessen his interruption he said, "I'm sorry to bother you this early in the morning but our taps don't work. Rachel was in the middle of her shower then suddenly there was no water."

Sam and Stephanie exchanged glances then Sam rose from the table. "Let's take a look, shall we?" Sam led the way as Rachel's adoring husband followed.

From their vantage point the three watched as Sam entered the cottage then reappeared a few moments later. He went behind the cottage then walked along the side as if looking for a leak or some sign of damage. Then he proceeded to follow the water line down the grassy slope to the lake. He stopped at a rock outcrop near the entrance of the boathouse.

His breakfast untouched Mike pushed his chair away from the table. "I'll go and see," he said. "It looks like Sam found something."

At the rock by the boathouse Sam was kneeling and examining the half-buried hose. It led from the cottage to the lake and was the source of water for the building. "It's broken," he explained as Mike joined him.

Mike knelt down and examined the break. "It doesn't look worn," he ran his hand along the jagged edge, "but it doesn't look like a knife cut either.

Jennifer watched from the side window and when the men didn't return, she got up to join them. Stephanie

110

although wanting to join them decided to get ready for her breakfast guests instead. A glimpse of sunlight shot out from between the clouds. The dark grey blanket had broken up now into patches of many clouds. And with the sunlight came the mosquitoes. Jennifer swatted as she walked along the path her runners squishing with each step, soaked now from a few unmissed puddles.

"I might have a larger piece in the boathouse," said Sam. They were discussing a way to splice the broken hose back together.

"Shall I go and get Tyler?" she offered.

Sam looked up from the problem at hand. "It's his morning off today. He went to his grandmother's last night."

"But I just saw him this morning not too long ago." Jennifer was puzzled. "I'm sure I saw him, he was standing right here by the boathouse," her voice trailed off to a whisper, "then when I called to him, he went inside."

Mike and Sam were busy discussing the hose and neither paid attention to her final account. "This shouldn't take long," assured Sam when his guest came and joined them. "I have a larger piece of hose and glue so I can splice it back together right now."

The worried husband, relieved at the news hurried back inside to tell his wife. Rachel was standing at the cottage window, her hair wrapped in a white towel and wearing a lush white bathrobe.

Jennifer's thoughts were racing. She was sure she had seen Tyler this morning. But then so what, perhaps he had decided not to go to his grandmother's. Maybe he planned to go over for a few hours after breakfast. Then what was he doing by the boathouse? "Sam, I have to check on something," said Jennifer.

Retracing her steps past the dining room she took the path that forked to the rear of the building where two small cabins stood side by side across from the laundry room and Jennifer's bedroom. Tyler's cabin was the furthest one, near to the parked cars by the office. Hoping to find Tyler up and about and provide some sense to what she thought she had seen this morning, she climbed the three steps and knocked on the screen door. When her knock was not answered Jennifer knocked again on the solid wooden door that was usually ajar but was closed now. No answer.

Confused by the mornings events Jennifer sat down on the cabin steps. She was sure she had seen Tyler and he was by the boathouse door, close to where the hose had been broken. Why had he hurried off unless he didn't want to be seen near the hose. Jennifer hoped, knew, what she was thinking couldn't be true. As she sat thinking about Tyler, the little she knew of him, her accusing thoughts didn't make sense. Why would he do such a thing?

A chipmunk darted along the edge of the building his cheeks filled with some delicious finds. It disappeared down a hole beneath the office window. Sam's truck was a few feet away parked where it had been sitting for the last few days. It had been backed in so that from where she sat its long scrape along the driver's side was visible. Soon to be erased at a paint shop next week. She stared at the vehicle. Something wasn't right. It took a couple of seconds then she realized Sam's truck had been vandalized.

Along the undercarriage, wires that were normally clamped and secured now hung lower than normal. The windows were rolled up and tinted yet Jennifer could see now that part of the roof interior, the head liner, hung down above the steering wheel. No, not vandalized, searched. She had been right about the owl. Someone had been there.

Just as Jennifer was about to get up from her vantage point on the steps, she heard a car driving in which parked across from the cabin in the guests parking lot area. Gathering up bags from his front seat Tyler made his way across the road toward his cabin. He stopped for a moment to adjust the heavy grocery bags in his hands then seeing Jennifer on his cabin steps he smiled, "What's up?"

The grocery bags were from a store at the far end of town. There was no way Tyler could have been here when Jennifer thought she saw him. She decided to trust her instincts and confront Tyler. She wanted Tyler to somehow clear up her suspicions. "I thought I saw you earlier this morning. I wanted to check something out but I forgot you were away 'til noon."

Tyler sat two bags down on the cabin step while he opened the door with his free hand. Jennifer picked up the bags of groceries and followed Tyler into the one room cabin. Setting the groceries on the sink counter he took the remaining bags from Jennifer. Then a puzzled look came over him and he turned to Jennifer. "When did you say you saw me?"

"About an hour ago."

"Where?"

"By the boathouse entrance just before a water line broke near number seven." She used a less incriminating description of the broken pipe.

He gave her another puzzled look. "Jen, I've been at my grandmothers since last night. She didn't have many chores for me to do so I came back early." The puzzled lines in his face suddenly smoothed and a sudden knowing look came over him. "And the person you saw looked like me?" he asked.

"Could have been your twin," she answered.

He slowly unpacked his beverages, snacks and cabin necessities, his thoughts racing.

Suddenly Jennifer remembered about Sam's truck. "Tyler, I almost forgot, Sam's truck has been searched." This latest revelation shocked him from his trance and he turned to question Jennifer.

"How do you know?"

"I'll show you." Together they went outside and Jennifer sat back in her previous position on the steps. Tyler, curious as to what she was doing joined her. "Look," she said, "the wires below the truck, and the head liner in the truck, you can see it from here." Then she lowered her voice, "Last night I thought someone might be back here. And do you remember the other night after the smoking chimney when I thought I heard an animal, it must have been him cutting the brake line."

Tyler regained his puzzled look. "I don't get it, why would someone want to search Sam's truck?"

Jennifer, after a moment's thought decided to trust Tyler with the earlier discussion. "We think someone is watching the lodge. He was in cottage twelve last night. All these accidents that keep happening around the lodge, we think it's deliberate." Tyler didn't reply but wore his usual serious expression. He seemed to be thinking, trying to piece the incidents together.

The chipmunk hopping along the edge of the lodge after another hunting expedition, paused to glance at the newest member of the cabin steps. His motion caught Jennifer's eye and she smiled as he scurried toward his underground chamber. He dove down the hole that was hidden from predators by a weathered tree root. Almost immediately he was back up peeking out checking the surrounding area before resuming his explorations.

Tyler now had seen the small creature and sat silently with Jennifer watching it still thinking about what Jennifer had told him. The small striped chipmunk scampered over to the back of Sam's truck. He jumped up onto the bumper then looked at Tyler and Jennifer as if begging for the delicious peanuts that cottagers always gave him. He came along the bumper cautiously until he reached the edge of the licence plate. Standing on his hind legs he stretched up to the top of the A on the MISHA plate. It had taken this small animal most of yesterday afternoon and part of the morning to pull out the soft white string that lodged itself behind the licence plate and now with a few more tugs he would have another soft piece of material for his burrow.

Jennifer and Tyler watched mesmerized by his effort. At last, the string was loose and the chipmunk gave it a final tug, but now it was stuck. Something stopped the string from coming free. After a few futile attempts the chipmunk temporarily gave up and sat back again on the bumper looking at them as if asking for help. "Oh," said Jennifer. "that's so cute, I'll pull it out for him." As soon

115

as Jennifer moved, the chipmunk leaped from the bumper and scurried back toward his hole. Jennifer picked up the end of the frayed string and gave it a tug. She tried twice then finally pulled it firmly enough that it broke free from its tether behind the plate. There was a sound of metal on metal as the string came loose. A key bounced off the indented bumper then landed on the ground hitting a small rock near Jennifer's feet. The bit of string fell limply to the ground as Jennifer kneeled to pick up the key. Having watched the pulling contest, amused by Jennifer's attempt, Tyler came to her side.

"What is it?"

"A key! But why was it stuck behind the plate?"

"What have you got there?" asked Sam. With their repairs completed he and Mike had wondered where Jennifer had gone. The chipmunk daring to return to the truck while humans were there swiftly picked up his treasure and returned to his home.

Jennifer held out the key for inspection. "Your truck has been torn apart too, searched by someone."

The father from number six passed them on his way to the car park area and waved his good morning. He was ready for another great day of fishing.

After glancing at the truck's cab, Mike spoke softly reminding the others that they should go and talk of this somewhere where they wouldn't be seen or overheard. Sam resisted inspecting his vehicle and nodded in agreement.

The father was careful not to open his door too wide as he reached in to retrieve a forgotten hat. Someone had parked their blue Chrysler a little too close to his driver's side.

By 8:30 they were all back in the dining room. The last of the breakfast guests was leaving having first picked up a picnic lunch for his party. Stephanie quickly cleared away the last of the dishes then joined her companions at a table for six.

Sam fingered the key in his hand. "This is obviously very important to someone," he said, "and I do believe we now have something more substantial, worth involving the police." Everyone nodded in agreement.

Tyler, with his usual serious expression sat next to Mike and up to now hadn't commented upon the discovery or the intruder. "Boss, I've got some work to finish up," Tyler pushed his chair away from the table, "I'll be near the boathouse." He gave Jennifer a knowing look as he left.

"I'll be right back," said Jennifer. She caught up to Tyler near the humming bird feeder. Once beside him, he stopped and faced her. She could see the determination in his face. "What is it, what's wrong?"

"That wasn't me this morning, I have a hunch but I have to find out for myself."

"Let me help."

"Not yet," he insisted.

Jennifer watched as Tyler followed the path to the boathouse entrance. She felt badly. Maybe she shouldn't have said anything to him about this morning. She hoped she hadn't sounded accusing. Her suspicions didn't seem important now.

Contrary to what he had said, Tyler did not intend to work. Instead, he quickened his steps toward the boathouse. Once inside he looked around then found a spot mid-way along the wall, across from the tool bench, a place where motors that needed repair were placed on upright stands, a place in shadow, where he could stand and not be seen from either entrance. He waited.

"Sam's called the police," said Stephanie. "They said they would be here in a few hours."

Sam was still fingering the key, "Why don't you two go out on the lake for a while. We can tell the police anything they need to know."

"I'll pack you a lunch," offered Stephanie.

It was a welcomed relief from the stress of the morning. "Thanks, Stephanie, I'd like that." Jennifer turned to Mike and smiled, "Well, what do you think?"

"I'd enjoy your company; besides I don't think much will happen before dusk."

"Shall we take the guide boat Sam?" asked Mike.

"Yes, it should have a full tank, but you can check with Tyler."

During the past hour the clouds had cleared and the threat of rain was postponed to a later date. While Jennifer went to change, Mike decided to get the boat ready and meet her at the main dock in front of the dining room. From his hiding place against the wall, Tyler watched as Mike backed the fourteen-foot guide boat out of the boathouse.

Chapter 11

The fog had dissipated now and the lake water was smooth except for the occasional ripple caused by a sporadic westerly breeze. Jennifer was ready, waiting for Mike on the main dock. She had changed into a swim suit for tanning and layered that with a tank top, hooded wind breaker and her new green slacks that unzipped at the legs creating three different lengths. In her hand she held one of Sam's light jackets. Stephanie's picnic lunch and drinks were packed in a thermos bag and sat on the dock next to Jennifer.

Thoughts of the morning events raced through her mind. She couldn't help feeling like she had let Tyler down. Mike manoeuvred the wooden boat next to Jennifer leaving the motor on low. "You look deep in thought," said Mike. She smiled.

The lodge guests were beginning to stir. The two chubby children from cottage two hurried down the path from their cottage, to the main dock. With fishing rods in tow, they made themselves comfortable at the edge of the dock splashing the water with their bare feet. "We saw a big fish here last night," said the youngest. They had raced their father from the cottage who now joined his two eager fishermen.

"Good morning," he said. He was armed with his own rod and reel and a wooden worm bucket.

Jennifer smiled, "Good luck," she said as she accepted Mike's hand and stepped into the guide boat. She took up her previous position and faced Mike. The picnic lunch was secured behind her under the seat. Both were quiet as they left the docking area. They passed the towering painted rock and for a while kept to the left past the flat rock and her encounter with the pike. Once past the rock and into the main channel, Mike slowed the motor to a crawl and broke the silence.

"Thank you for the jacket," he smiled. "I wish now that I had my camera with me. The light is perfect this morning." Sensing something was wrong he finally stopped the motor. "Okay, what is it?"

"I didn't tell Sam what happened with Tyler today." Her eyes looked pleadingly at his. "Maybe I should have said something." Jennifer confessed her suspicions from earlier this morning and her conversation with Tyler later. She concluded with her uneasiness at Tyler's last comments as he walked towards the boathouse.

"I didn't see him working in the boathouse," said Mike. Then offered, "Maybe he decided to take care of other chores first." Jennifer looked deep in thought. "Don't take things too seriously," he continued, "I'm sure everything will work out okay."

Jennifer nodded slowly in agreement.

"Well, Miss Jennifer," trying to lighten the mood, "where shall we go on this beautiful day?"

Jennifer looked at the map she now unfolded from her jacket pocket. "If we go along the main channel, we'll pass a large island on our right. Turn right there then follow the channel until we come to a break in the shore on our left. We should see an Inukshuk marker on the point. We turn left there. Shortly after that we'll reach the narrows."

Mike smiled seeing her enthusiasm returning. "Very well. Let's see how fast this boat will go." Mike started up the motor and gradually turned the throttle up. Jennifer pulled her hood up over her head and held on as the boat cut a path through the rippled water.

As they turned right past the large island Jennifer noticed a boat in the shallows between the island and the far shore. There were two people in the boat and although she couldn't tell who the occupants were, she was able to see the painted white animal print at the prow of the boat indicating it belonged to the Painted Rock Lodge. Probably the reclusive couple from cottage one. Boats on the five-mile lake usually belonged to the lodge or guests who had their own boat, but sometimes to locals who had public access at a ramp near the far end of the lake.

After several minutes they reached the Inukshuk marker. A large peninsula of rock jutted out from the mainland and on a part that was furthest into the lake sat a huge rock person like formation, one of the main markers shown on Jennifer's map.

Veering left Mike slowed down. Past the stone marker the water way led them past several small islands surrounded by weed beds. A floating white plastic jug showed where a rotting tree projected out of the water. Cautiously Mike manoeuvred the boat between the islands. Jennifer had moved to the front of the boat now and leaned out watching for unseen rocks that might hit the motor as they went by.

"This looks like a good spot," she said. "Weed beds are great for pickerel and dare I say, pike." Her mood had changed now and her mind was off of the recent events of the morning.

Sheltered among the islands they decided to drift and not anchor. Mike handed Jennifer the rod that had been in its usual place while he pondered over what lure to use. "What about a jig?"

"Sounds good." Jennifer liked using a jig. Bobbing the lure up and down among the weeds gave you something to do and made you feel like you were actually fishing instead of sitting and waiting for a nibble.

After attaching the white wiggly bait, she tossed it over the side. The jig head was also a weight so it sank quickly to the bottom. Jennifer raised it up off the bottom as she reeled in then started bobbing the rod tip up and down in long strokes which gave the jig its fish attracting motion.

Jennifer's first nibble was a successful bite. "I've got one!" she cried. "It feels like a big one!"

Mike unhooked the net from the other side of the boat and prepared to help haul in her catch. By now Jennifer had the fish near the surface. "Oh, it's just a sunfish," she said disappointed. "But it sure felt big."

"Well, it's a big sunfish." said Mike. "They're actually quite tasty and make a nice meal if you catch enough." He looked at the dangling fish. "Would you like me to take it off for you?"

Jennifer looked at the plump brilliantly coloured fish hanging heavily from her line. 'Please, I'm afraid it may have swallowed the hook."

There were needle nosed pliers in the kit for just such an occasion. Mike slowly detached the hook from inside the fish's mouth. "It's not too bad," he said as he released the fish over the side. "When I'm fishing alone, I usually squeeze the barbs on the hook so they're closed. I find it's less stressful on both me and the fish when you're trying to release a catch."

The pliers reminded Jennifer of the duck rescue and she smiled. She was seeing the same caring gentle side of Mike and she liked that.

A motor boat whizzed past the stone marker on its way to the far end of the lake. Jennifer recognized the boat and hoped Glen Malloy and Derek Kerr would continue to head up the main channel.

"Do you want to try here again?" he asked. It was getting warmer and the sky had cleared now leaving only a few wispy clouds in the west.

"Let's go on through to the other lake. We can have lunch in another hour."

The thought of the beautiful breakfast left sitting on his plate when he went to help Sam came to mind and reminded him how hungry he was. "Lunch sounds good. We can find a nice island with a sandy beach."

They went on further up the water way veering to the right as they came to the narrows, a passage way, linking the two larger lakes together. Watching from the bow Jennifer pointed the optimum route until they were well clear of any rocks that might damage the motor. Just past the narrows the waters widened up. On the right was a rocky outcrop, that with its one tall pine could have qualified as a small island. Surrounding it just under the water's surface were large flat rocks. A weed bed wafted under the water between the island and the shore. A good place to try. Jennifer gave Mike the rod for a while and watched contentedly as he cast close to the shore.

It was Mike who brought up the conversation with Tyler again. "You told Tyler that you saw him at the boathouse?"

"Yes, but he said he'd been at his grandmother's and he was just getting back from town."

The weeds broke the surface closer to the shore and Mike's last cast had gone a little too close. "I'm caught."

Sitting in the middle seat Jennifer was near the oars. "I'll row," she offered, "that way you can get close enough to pull it out without losing the lure."

The boat turned slightly as she rowed in a forward motion not wanting her back facing the spot she was aiming for. "Good, got it!" he said, winding in the line quickly. Then switching the topic, "If it wasn't Tyler, who was it you saw at the boathouse?"

Jennifer rowed backwards facing Mike at the back of the boat. "I don't know."

"Maybe it was our guy from number twelve?" pondered Mike. "But how the key fits in with the sabotage at the lodge I can't figure."

They spent the next hour fishing at various weed beds they came upon. At times they sat together leaning against the centre seat and just talked. They had come quite a distance from the narrows by the time they decided to have lunch and stopped opposite a large beach on a stretch of mainland. It looked inviting, its overhanging trees providing some shade from the hot sun.

The drone of a motor in the distance caught their attention. Coming back from the furthest end of the lake were Mr. Nelson and his English fisherman. On their way back to the lodge for lunch, they slowed briefly as they went by. John Taylor gave an enthusiastic wave and a "What a great day!" from the front of the boat stretching his hands out to show the size of a fish he had caught.

Both Jennifer and Mike laughed. "I'm glad he caught something," she said. "Well, let's have our lunch."

"Very well, Miss Jennifer."

They were drifting now and the waves of the passing boat pulled them along the waterway. "We'll tie up over there," he nodded to the end of the beach where a large cedar tree was bent over the water. Jennifer re-positioned herself in the middle of the seat while Mike started the motor. But the motor wouldn't start. Mike tried again but nothing happened. "That's funny, we had a full tank coming out." Mike leaned toward the back of the boat and checked the gas gauge. It said full. "Something's not right," he said, and took hold of the gas tank handle tilting it to see how much gas was left. There was only a trickle.

He had been standing there for almost two hours now and it was almost time for him to be officially back at work. Maybe his suspicions were wrong and accidents that had happened at the lodge were just that, accidents. The sun had slowly illuminated the lake side of the boathouse making Tyler's hiding spot even darker. A tiny brown spider had joined him and was now crawling up and down a motor handle as if deciding whether to begin a web or not. A noise at the entrance caught his attention. At first, he thought it was a guest seeking assistance but he stayed quiet and kept his hiding spot. A man was standing there his face difficult to see with the light behind him. He walked cautiously into the boathouse checking once around first. He stood opposite Tyler now at the tool table and didn't appear to realize he was being watched. His back still to Tyler the man looked again toward the entrance then moved toward the end of the tool table near the worm fridge. With his left hand he unplugged the fridge.

"Nice try, cousin."

Eddy snatched a wrench from the tool table and turned to confront his cousin. "I wish you hadn't seen that, Tyler." He looked from side to side as if trying to decide which escape route to take. "I was doing this for our family," he protested. "You know this should be our land not theirs, and it would have been if they hadn't bought it first!" He was clenching the wrench tighter now. His eyes flitting back and forth from Tyler to the lake entrance.

All day Tyler had been torn between family and friendship, doing the right thing or turning a blind eye. And now he knew he had done what was right.

Sam stood in the doorway with his rifle pointing towards Eddy. "You can put the wrench down now," he said.

Eddy threw the wrench to the earthen floor where it gouged a divot in the ground.

It was close to 2:30 before Sam and Stephanie became concerned. There was no sign of the guide boat. Mr. Taylor had seen Jennifer and Mike near a pleasant beach and assured Stephanie that all seemed well but now the clouds were gathering and there was a distant rumbling of thunder from the west. The water in the lodge's sheltered bay had not yet shown signs of waves but the water around Mike and Jennifer's guide boat was now showing small white caps as the wind gusts grew stronger. With the rumbling from the west came the grey clouds and threat of rain. Seagulls that had sat contentedly on small rock outcrops now circled and screeched.

They had been drifting for a while before getting caught up on a sand bar on an island south of the beach they had intended to land on. It was a long way back to the lodge but Jennifer took comfort in knowing that someone had seen them earlier and if help came, they would probably start searching near the beach area first. The island they were stuck on was not large enough to provide much cover in case of a storm so Mike and Jennifer had decided to stay in the boat. But where they were now, provided no shelter from the gusts of wind and waves and their wooden boat was being buffeted against the rocks embedded in the sandy bottom. If they could land on the east shore of the mainland somewhere or a larger island they would be sheltered from the westerly gusts.

Mike decided to try. They would use the oars and after pushing themselves free from the sandy trap, would attempt to row back to the middle of the waterway against the wind and try to direct the boat to a more favourable spot. Sitting on either side of the boat, Mike and Jennifer each pushed down with their oar and together slid the boat off its sandy trap. Once back in moving water Mike returned to the back seat and used his oar as a rudder to steer. The dead motor held tightly provided some direction as well and using both, the westerly wind carried them further up the lake. Approaching two islands on their right Mike was able to direct their boat between the two. "We'll have to row!" he decided.

Crouching low so she wouldn't tip the boat in this wind, Jennifer helped place her oar on its holder. Mike traded places with her as he installed his oar then began rowing. Jennifer tied her jacket hood securely. Against the wind he managed to manoeuvre their boat into the sheltered bay of the larger island. Without the wind pulling at their boat Mike was able to finally row to shore. Wild rice hugged the perimeter of the shore and flattened as the bottom of their boat glided across. Unlike their previous island this one had several trees and rocky outcrops and shrub like growth covered the entire surface.

Mike jumped out after setting the oars back inside the boat and pulled their boat up onto the small sandy area. "We'll be okay now," said Mike. "Even if it gets really bad, we can use the boat for shelter until someone comes."

Jennifer gave him a reassuring smile, but in reality, even if someone did see them earlier the weather was too risky for a search, especially in another lodge boat equipped with the same size motor. No, they would be alright here. She looked at Mike, his hair loose now blowing in the wind, his jacket unzipped and flapping wildly. He was wet up to his knees as he tied the boat to an extended tree branch, but he was smiling. He ran back, splashing, and lifted the food bag Jennifer offered him. Then he reached out for her hand. "Milady?"

Jennifer laughed, for a moment forgetting their predicament and remembering their last time together on a beach. Together they splashed through the waves and ran to a treed area of the beach. Mike had thrown two life jackets down on the sand and here the two sat huddled together watching and waiting. Mike put his arm around her and gave her shoulders a squeeze. "Isn't this neat," he said. "Who would have thought a month ago I'd be on an island in the middle of an Ontario lake miles from anywhere with my arms around a beautiful woman during a thunderstorm."

She laughed, "Yes, and on a Tuesday too." They both laughed.

Chapter 12

The Ontario Provincial Police officers took their statements and left with Eddy in the back seat of their car. Sam decided not to press charges after Tyler had assured him that Eddy's father as native band leader would deal with him. He felt badly and was embarrassed by his cousin's behaviour. He had confessed to Sam that he had been suspicious after finding the dead animal in the fireplace pipe. It had been stuffed in and hadn't gone in on its own.

Sam was glad that Tyler had confided in him and together they had set the ambush for the person causing the 'accidents' at the lodge. Eddy had confessed to setting the trap for Sam and all the other incidents that had been plaguing the lodge in the hopes that Stephanie and Sam would become frustrated and sell, but he denied any knowledge of the truck mishaps. Which meant there was another intruder, a far more dangerous one, in the camp.

The storm had been growing and more threatening since noon. Stephanie had watched to see that all lodge guests were accounted for. The guide boat was the only lodge boat missing and Glen Malloy upon arriving back with his companion agreed to go back out and check for Jennifer and Mike. Glen Malloy had a 60-horse motor on his sixteen-foot fishing boat which could stand up to the waves of the lake and was also much faster than the lodge motors. John Taylor who had seen the couple earlier offered to go along and guide them to the sandy beach past the narrows. But for now, rescue would have to wait. The storm gave no indication of easing up soon.

Huddled together Mike and Jennifer sat watching the lake. They'd found better shelter against a large pink coloured granite rock which curved slightly against a pine tree. It was gusting continuously now with the whitecaps creating a milky froth along the shore.

"I'm still hungry, what about lunch," suggested Mike.

Jen laughed. "We're in a storm, wet, cold, miles from home and you want to eat."

"Well, we can at least look and see what Stephanie made for us. Besides once the rain starts, I don't want to be totally wet, cold, miles from home and hungry too."

"Okay," she grinned, then opened the thermal bag which held an assortment of picnic necessities, plates, cups, food and juice containers.

"This looks good." Jen smiled as she offered Mike half of a tuna salad sandwich. A gust of wind whisked away the plastic wrapping before she could grab it.

He sighed, "This is good!" He made little groan noises as he devoured a second half in record time. There was a strange yellow colour in the sky and as they sat there eating, suddenly the waters in front of their refuge began churning. It was if thousands of little fish were huddled in one small area all jumping frantically. There was a loud roaring of the wind and the wild rice flattened, then suddenly the water rose in that spot forming a ten-foot column above the surface. It lasted only a few seconds then fell dramatically back into the water. The churning had stopped and just as suddenly the winds died down. Both sat there amazed. "That was fantastic!" said Mike. "We'll probably never see that again in our lifetime," then he shook his head, "and I didn't have my camera."

"What was it?" Jennifer kept her arms around Mike's waist.

"A waterspout."

"It was a little scary," she admitted, "like a small tornado sucking up the water." He tightened his embrace. Now that it was all over, she smiled.

There was quiet and then all of a sudden, the sky opened up and a torrent of extra-large drops rained over them stinging as they fell. It rained steadily for the remainder of the day. Gusty north westerly winds and waves buffeted their island shore line. Mike and Jennifer had pulled the boat ashore once it seemed that there was no immediate end in sight. Mike unhooked the motor from the gas tank and released it from the back mounting board and together they raised the boat up so it rested overturned against the pink granite outcrop. As least now, even though they were soaked they had some protection from the pelting rain. Thunder added to the sound of rain hitting the wooden hull. Lightening cracked above their tiny island. "One, one thousand, two," said Jennifer, then abandoned her counting when a thunderous boom shook the air.

Huddled together under the wooden shelter they sat on soggy life preservers and shared the remainder of Stephanie's packed lunch.

"Here you go." Jennifer handed Mike the last of the sandwiches. Deciding to save their hot thermos of coffee for later they each had a cranberry drink, a nectarine, and a slice of banana cake.

"What a wonderful picnic," he exclaimed, extending his right arm beyond the sheltering edge of the overturned boat and thus rinsing off the nectarine juice in the rain.

Jennifer laughed and followed his example then wiped her wet hands on her jeans. Hidden from the storm in their shelter the darkened sky gave the impression of night fall. The rain had no intention of ending but thankfully the wind had died down so the rain fell straight.

The granite rock, warmed from the morning sun was now cooling. Rivulets of rain water had streamed from the exposed top and ran down the flat face and under their makeshift cushions.

"We might be here a while," said Mike, "so let's try to be a bit more comfortable." Mike outlined his idea and together the dragged the oars from their sandy resting place on the beach.

Using the oars as spades Mike and Jennifer dug small ditches along the length of the boat on either side which discouraged the rain water from entering their shelter. Instead, it flowed into the small trench then down past the boat toward the beach.

Jennifer made a third ditch across the front of the rock and joined it into the two side depressions. "There," she said satisfied. "We're on our own little sandy island." Mike smiled at her efforts then helped her dig the channel a little deeper to prevent overflow.

The hours passed and the storm had no intention of easing up. The wind would stir up sporadically giving the storm a renewed intensity then die down again giving a false hope to the two marooned boaters.

It was almost six o'clock and the damp air was cooling. For the last half hour, she had sat resting against Mike's side, his left arm encircling her keeping her warm.

"Do you think it'll stop before dark?" she asked, already anticipating his answer.

"Probably not," he confessed, "so we may be here all night."

Jennifer gave a shiver. She looked at the assemblage of wood Mike had the for thought to gather, just in case. The storm would have made the wood impossible to burn but now if the rain stopped, they could have a small fire. It sat piled on the sand under the wide stern of the boat. There had been lots of driftwood and broken branches scattered along the beach edge where it met the shrubbery and other small plants of the island. "It's too bad we can't start a fire now; it's going to feel cold tonight in these wet clothes."

"Don't worry, I'll keep you warm," and he surrounded her with his arms and held her close.

She could hear his heart beating and like a little lost puppy she felt safe beside the reassuring sound. "I know," she said softly. There was something about Mike that made you feel everything would be okay. His constant optimism and air of efficiency perhaps. She leaned back a bit and looked up into his smiling face.

"I'm having fun, aren't you?" he asked.

"Yes actually. It's a wonderful adventure. I just hope Stephanie and Sam aren't too worried about us."

Mike leaned over and gave her a kiss on the forehead. "I'm sure they know we would have taken cover."

"They probably took cover," Sam had tried to reassure Stephanie. "There're plenty of places for them to pull the boat up and weather out the storm." Stephanie gave him a weak smile. "John Taylor did say they were near a large beach out of the wind and," he continued, "Glen Malloy said he would take his boat and look if the wind died down before dark".

Knowing it wasn't safe even with a 40-horse motor Sam had declined an earlier search. The lake was known for its unpredictable north westerly winds and today was just such an example. Darkness presented a different problem though. The lake was low this summer and many rock formations that would normally not be a problem now waited just below the surface for an unsuspecting boater. Tyler had been eager to go on his own using one of the lodge boats but turned back frustrated when his boat had difficulty getting past the grey rock face with its painted animals. No, they would wait until it was safe before sending out a search vessel.

"How long have you been a photographer?" asked Jennifer. Mike had changed his position and now leaned back against the assembled wood pile while still sitting on a life preserver and Jennifer curled up at his side with his arms around her.

"Most of my life, actually. When I was eight my parents gave me my grandparents old Brownie and I soon became the family photographer. I saved up for a good manual camera when I was fifteen, complete with a teleconverter and two lenses. Over the years I found I had a talent for it and three years ago when my boss needed someone to go to China I volunteered. The rest is history," he adjusted his shoulder against a jutting branch, "Preserving moments in time, that's what I do." He smiled, "You'd make a pretty picture right now."

Jennifer ran her fingers through her tousled hair, "Well in that case, I'm glad you don't have your camera."

It was dusk or by Mike's watch it should have been. Grey clouds covered the early night and it was difficult to tell whether the sun had set or not. Finally, the rain stopped so they could attempt a fire. For the last half hour Mike had been preparing the wood for that eventuality. Survival tools were part of the guide boats equipment. Among the fishing gear Mike had found a small hatchet, matches in a water tight container, a fillet knife for cleaning fish and a flare gun which unfortunately he doubted could be seen back at the lodge.

"Well," said Mike, pleased with his survival skills, "we have everything we need to make it through the night."

The wind was a soft breeze now creating ripples that caressed the shore line. Applying his chimney pipe concept Mike layered rocks creating a dry base for his fire. Using sliced bark and shavings from small branches Mike started the fire. It caught on his first try, so carefully he added smaller twigs and branches until it was in no danger of fizzling out. From this rocky bed air could sweep up from the base adding fuel to the small flames.

While Mike was busy tending the fire Jennifer retrieved the fishing rod and lures from their place in the boat. He smiled as she stood knee deep in water and attempted to cast out beyond the sandy bottom.

"Good thinking," he shouted.

Jennifer had chosen a night lure, one that made noise as it was worked along the water surface antagonizing the fish, making them strike. Fishing after a storm wasn't usually the most productive time but she would try anyway. The water calmed and its surface flattened reminding her of the times she and Stephanie took the boat out beyond the shore and swam in the lake at Uncle Terry's cottage. She tried a hula popper, pulling it along in small jerks which created a popping sound but with no luck. After giving it a fair chance Jennifer switched to a brown rattling mouse. There were weeds past the sandy bottom and to the left of a rocky outcrop that she had seen yesterday before the storm. She walked to the far end of their tiny beach and cast out beyond the rocks. The mouse had a taut line that attached to the tip of the hook from its base so that the lure passed over weeds and rocks preventing potential snags. She could hear the tiny rattle as she lifted the lure out of the water ready to cast again.

Mike had finished prepping his fire now and after adding a few larger pieces of wood, sat on a nearby flat rock and watched Jennifer's attempts. He marvelled at her skill with a rod and reel and enjoyed just watching her. Jennifer's wet top was off, and like her long pants was laid out across the hull of the boat. Jennifer was in her swim suit now and he didn't mind the view. She was a beautiful woman.

Pulling the lure in spurts to mimic a mouse swimming, Jennifer felt a tug. The line was heavy and felt like she was pulling in a small drifting log. She figured the protective wire must have come off the hook allowing the barb to snag.

"Can you use some more wood?" she called.

Mike laughed, "We'll mount it and keep it for a souvenir," he said.

Jennifer laughed, "At least I'm not stuck," she said, "It's coming along slowly."

Then it broke the water. A large fish jumped and smacked the surface before diving back under. What she had thought was a drifting log was actually a largemouth bass that had been hanging around the rocky outcrop. Jennifer kept her rod up and her line tight. If it jumped and was still on the line after that Jennifer knew she had a good chance of landing it. She backed up slowly, careful of her footing so she wouldn't stumble. All she would need to lose her catch was to let the line slacken off.

Mike joined her at the water's edge. "It's got to be a big one!" he shouted excitedly. He resisted the urge to offer help and watched as Jennifer stepped backwards out of the water and up the sandy beach. Her rod bent almost double now but she was keeping the pressure even and slowly the fish was pulled in towards shore.

Once it zigzagged and Mike could hear the drag whining as the fish made one last effort to get away. Then finally it was on the shore flopping. "That was great!" Mike noticed the hook caught in the fish's lip. "Any slack and he would be a free fish right now." Mike held up her catch. "Fish for supper, Milady?"

Jennifer smiled and although she usually preferred to release her catches, she was feeling the pangs of hunger. She looked sadly at the gasping fish.

"I know," said Mike sympathetically, "I'll take care of it," he offered. "Why don't you spread your clothes out near the fire while I prepare supper." He could see she was shivering now.

Mike roasted the fish on secured branches careful not to set them alight over the open fire. "Well, it's good to know I have a woman with me who's a good provider," he teased. "We won't go hungry on this island," he

138

grinned in anticipation of their tasty meal. The fish, nicely browned was cut up on a rock slab. Mike offered the first piece to Jennifer on a leafy plate.

Jennifer smiled at his enthusiasm, then remembered the thermos, "We have coffee too!" she said, reaching into Stephanie's picnic bag. "And a chocolate bar, that I sort of forgot to mention earlier." she said the latter part quietly then looked at Mike waiting for a response.

"Fish, coffee and chocolate. This is turning out to be a gourmet meal," he said, smiling. After an initial serving each, Mike removed as much meat as he could from the fish skeleton and shared it with Jennifer.

It was pitch black yet it must have been starting to clear for the first star of the evening appeared above them increasingly followed by others as the clouds gave way to a bright sky. Jennifer had never sat out during the night to look at the stars but now she awed at their number. It was ten-thirty now and they would have to spend the night together on their small rocky island.

Jennifer's three-layer pants were nylon and dried quickly by the fire propped up on one of two stick tepee formations. Her top and Mike's shirt hung from a cross stick held up by the tepees. Her hair was still damp but she began to feel warmer after her meal.

Together they shared the coffee, drinking alternately from the thermos cup. They sat side by side now against the middle seat of the guide boat. Mike had righted it, then together they dragged it from its spot by the granite rock over to its new position by the fire. Jennifer divided up the chocolate squares and between sips of coffee fed Mike one from his share. The boat was dry and they would have a dry place to sleep until morning. Four orange life preservers were taking their time drying near the fire but with luck would be dry enough to use as pillows later in the evening.

The fire lasted long enough to dry their clothing and eventually the life preservers. It had been a long day and both had had little sleep the night before. It was eleven thirty by the time the fire died out as there was not enough dry wood to keep it going. Mike had used the last drops of gasoline to encourage a few wet logs to flame for a while but as they were both tired and didn't want to stay awake to tend to it, they decided to let it fade.

For some reason there were no mosquitoes on their island. Jennifer didn't know why but was grateful for their absence. The moon had fattened since their last beach supper and now it slowly reached up into the sky from behind the treed horizon of the large island across from their sandy beach. There was a sudden scream in the darkness then a scuffling at the water's edge on the far shore. A predator had found his evening meal. Jennifer wondered if their small island had similar animals and wished now that they had kept the fire going.

They decided to sleep across the width of the boat. Mike with his back against the side and Jennifer nestled in his arms in front of him. "Look! A shooting star," he observed. Jennifer was looking up and followed the distant light as it arched over them and fell beyond the horizon. She was looking at him now and he smiled back. His face was close to hers and he caressed her cheek with his lips. His arm under her head raised up and he found her lips and gave her a passionate kiss. "Did you make a wish, Miss Jennifer?"

She stared into his steel blue eyes, "I got my wish," she answered, then smiled. Jennifer reached up with her free arm and gently pulled him close. They embraced under another shooting star.

Chapter 13

Morning found them snuggled together in the belly of the guide boat. Dampness from the morning dew clung to the inner walls of the boat. It must have been close to five thirty as the sun was just starting to rise following the same path the moon had taken the evening before. The water surrounding their island was dead calm. An early morning mist hugged the water's surface obscuring the opposite shoreline. It felt as if they were alone on a prehistoric island. Jennifer had been awakened by the rustling of branches behind them. She thought of last night's hunt across the water then hearing nothing more dismissed it as a chipmunk searching for its breakfast.

She lay still next to a sleeping Mike and took a simple delight in watching him. He looked even younger when he was sleeping and she smiled thinking of their shared adventure. His eyes fluttered then opened. He saw Jennifer watching him then smiled warmly. "Good morning," he said softly. "How long have you been awake?"

"Not long."

The sun was shining through the trees of the mainland now and it felt warm. "It looks like a beautiful day," he observed, then sat up and stretched. Mike flinched as a muscle twitched in pain. "I don't think I'll make a habit of sleeping in the bottom of boats though." He stood up and stretched again. "How did you sleep?"

"Great," smiled Jennifer. "I had a wonderful pillow and I was nice and warm." Then she laughed at the stiffness in his body as he tried to loosen up.

"Oh, look!" Mike pointed to water in front of them. A ripple moved steadily causing a miniature triangular wake as it travelled.

"What is it?"

Mike was out of the boat now fascinated by the moving creature. "An otter maybe, or a snapping turtle." The animal had a blunt head raised as it swam. Mike clapped his hands together. Immediately the animal slapped the water with its tail then dove out of sight. "Looks like it's a beaver." They waited, watching for the animal to resurface and when it did it was well past them heading for a smaller outcrop to the right of their beach.

The sound of a motor in the distance drew their attention. Jennifer looked at Mike for an instant as neither moved. "They're not going to be able to see us here if they head down the main waterway." Mike ran to the front of their boat and began pushing. "Hurry, we'll have to row out into the open."

Jennifer ran to the stern and began pulling and lost her footing once as the boat was now being pushed out into the rice flattened water. Her pants were soaked once more but now the water felt warm in the morning air and she didn't mind trudging through the water again. Each took an oar and placed it in its holder then positioning herself on the back seat Mike pulled the oars along the surface of the shallow water until they were free of the beach then pulled harder back out into the water between the two islands.

Jennifer could just see the boat now. It had come through the narrows and was following the same route they had taken. Mike rowed hard until they had passed back between the two islands just out into the main water way. Jennifer waved. She could tell now that it was Glen Malloy's boat and next to the driver was a man in a yellow hat and jacket who acknowledged her wave with a beep of the horn. She was glad it was John Taylor and not Derek Kerr, who had declined the rescue in favour of John Taylor after complaining how early it was to get up.

It was John Taylor who saw them first and signalled to Glen Malloy to ease up and turn around after passing the sheltering island. After a brief explanation regarding the gas tank Mike tied up the guide boat to the back of Glen Malloy's fishing boat and the two huddled on the floor with a blanket to keep out of the wind's chill from the drive back.

John Taylor sat in one of the side chairs facing the two marooned boaters, beaming from ear to ear. Jennifer smiled imagining the stories he might tell, about his Canadian adventure. With the guide boat under tow, it took a while as the rescue boat followed the path they had taken back to the lodge. Jennifer recognized a few landmarks and traced their trip back with each turn of the boat. She could tell as they slowed and went through the narrows, then turned left towards the stone landmark. The Inukshuk's upper body was visible as they turned right slowly up the channel then left again as they headed toward the lodge past the flat rock. Glen Malloy slowed again as they approached the dark grey vertical wall of the painted figures then into the sheltered bay of the Painted Rock Lodge.

Jennifer and Mike sat up now on the back fishing platform of the boat and watched as cottagers, most still dressed in their night attire, swarmed around the main dock. With the lights on all night and the staff up and about, word had spread among the guests that Jennifer and Mike had been stranded by the storm though why they hadn't returned at the first sign of thickening clouds no one could have known. Some clapped as they saw the two safely returning. The two twins from cottage five waved from their dock and the two chubby children ran up and down the main dock in anticipation of the arrival. It reminded Jennifer of nature programs she had seen in her childhood about the far north where Inuit villagers would run out and greet an incoming supply plane as it landed then taxied to the shore.

Sam and Stephanie were on the main dock with Tyler and as Glen Malloy steered next to them Tyler pulled the rope that John Taylor tossed to him from the front and secured the boat to the right arm of the u-shaped dock. He saw the gas tank disconnected and the motor laying across the back of the boat and realized something had happened to prevent the two from returning on their own.

Mike discarded the blanket and helped Jennifer on to the dock and into the arms of a waiting Stephanie.

"I'm so glad you're all right," Stephanie said. "I couldn't sleep all night, worrying."

Jennifer gave her a second hug. "It wasn't that bad, really. Just a little cold and wet. I'm glad I wasn't out there alone though."

Mike thanked the two men again for their rescue efforts then joined Sam and Tyler on the dock. "Someone tampered with the gas tank. We got as far as the beach by the narrows then when the storm approached, we couldn't get back." Mike caught Sam and Tyler exchange glances.

"I'll take the guide boat back," offered Tyler. Tyler untied the guide boat then proceeded to row it back over to the boathouse.

Sam nodded then put his arm around Mike, "Come on, we'll catch you up over a hot breakfast."

He had heard the early morning commotion from his hiding place up on the hill. Last night had been a source of frustration for him. Light had illuminated the entire area around the main lodge including the parked truck. The lodge staff had been up most of the night milling around the office and dock areas. He now knew the reason for the all-night vigil and watched from the tree lined lake edge near cottage three as the rescued couple made their way into the lodge. As cottagers dispersed, he receded back into the woods that surrounded the vacant cottage. Hopefully tonight would be his chance. It had to be. He needed that key. A key that held his future and untold wealth if only he could get the bundle that contained the counterfeit plates now resting in a public locker waiting to be claimed.

The father who had caught the large pickerel approached Jennifer, "We're all glad you're safe and sound young lady. Everyone's been worried about you." Jennifer smiled her thanks and continued up the path to the dining room with Stephanie. Derek Kerr was just approaching the dining room windows. He waved then stopped as he was joined by Glen Malloy. Once inside the lodge dining room the two weary boaters sat together with Sam while

Stephanie hurried to fix a warm meal. "I need to get out of these wet clothes first," said Jennifer.

"Jennifer's right." Sam looked at Mike's wet jeans. "I have some clothes you can borrow," said Sam. "We've got time, I'll show you to our room."

Jennifer was the last to return to the breakfast table. Luckily no one was coming in for breakfast later, which meant Stephanie could rest for a while after they ate. Jennifer returned to her place next to Mike who was now dressed in some of Sam's borrowed clothes. Coffee had helped to keep everyone alert most of the night and now the machine was streaming out a new batch.

Curious but resisting the urge to ask until Stephanie had rejoined them with a large platter of bacon and eggs, Mike now inquired, "So what's been happening,"

Sam offered them each a warm drink then sat down before answering. "Just after you went out yesterday, Tyler had a confrontation with his cousin."

Tyler walked in just as Sam was explaining how Tyler had come to him and proposed the idea of setting an ambush in the boathouse, then he took up the explanation.

"Eddy admitted to being responsible for all the trouble we've been having around the lodge," said Tyler. "He'd wait until I was away fishing or at my grandmothers then would sneak around knowing that if he was seen the guests would probably think he was me."

"And I suppose he looks enough like you to be your twin," smiled Jennifer. Everything was clear to Jennifer now, and she gave Tyler a warm smile glad that her instincts had proven right.

"He even set the trap for Sam to step in." added Stephanie.

"But why?" asked Jennifer.

Tyler's look changed now and she could tell it was difficult for him to confess Eddy's reason. "He thought if things got bad enough Sam and Stephanie would give up and sell this place. My Uncle wanted to but it when the Semples put it up for sale but he was too late."

"What will happen to him now?" asked Mike, as he helped himself to more bacon strips.

Sam smiled at his appetite, "He went with the police shortly after we caught him in the boathouse. Tyler suggested to them that he be dealt with by the band council. I guess I'll wait and see if they want me to press charges."

Jennifer picked up the last piece of bacon after giving Mike a triumphant look. "Well, that's a great relief. Things should be a lot less hectic around here now."

"Not necessarily," continued Sam.

Jennifer swallowed before asking, "What do you mean?"

"He admitted to everything but said he had nothing to do with the truck being run off the road or the brakes failing."

Mike and Jennifer exchanged looks. Jennifer started to recall her incidents with Sam's truck. "That means there's someone else tampering with the truck."

"Yes," confirmed Sam, "but last night nothing more happened. We think it's because we had the place lit up like an airport runway and with us pacing around the grounds, he probably didn't have a chance.

"So, it looks like tonight is the night," suggested Mike.

148

"We think so. John Taylor has offered to help plan the stake out."

"Well, with a big evening coming up I think I'll go home and get a few hours of proper sleep."

Mike gave Jennifer's shoulders a squeeze as he got up from the table. "What time tonight?"

It was Stephanie who answered, "Come for supper. John Taylor will be among the guests and we can discuss our plans after."

"Supper it is then." He held the door open for Tyler who had decided he would work on getting the guide boat back in shape ready for tomorrow morning.

"Your emergency gear helped us out a great deal." Mike acknowledged to Tyler, who smiled at the compliment.

"I'm just glad Eddy's sabotage didn't cause serious injury to anyone."

With the jeep headed back up the lodge road Jennifer sat alone now with Stephanie and Sam each with an expectant expression on their face. Then Jennifer smiled, "He was a perfect gentleman."

"So, I guess all our worrying was unnecessary," started Stephanie, "you seemed to be in good hands."

"I know it should have been a scary ordeal but actually it was a fun adventure." Then she laughed to herself, "Probably because Mike is so positive. It's hard to have an ordeal with him around." She smiled remembering their wet picnic and sandy island. "Somehow he finds the good side of things."

"I'm glad you're alright. I tried to tell Stephanie you'd be okay." Standing behind Stephanie's chair Sam gave her a small hug. Then in a relieved tone, "Well that's all I needed to know. I'll be in the boathouse if you need me. I want to check out all the gas gauges just in case."

Since Eddy's arrest Sam and Tyler had found one motor that didn't work and one barbecue tank that was jammed up but checking the gas tank gauges up till now hadn't occurred to them.

Once alone the girls sat side by side contemplating the day's events. Stephanie had been proven right about her suspicions. "You were right all along," said Jennifer, then gave Stephanie a sympathetic smile, "it must have been frustrating for you when you weren't taken seriously."

"Well with Eddy no longer in camp we shouldn't have any more trouble, and I'm glad of that," admitted Stephanie, "but I'm also worried about tonight." She finished up the last of her coffee before continuing. "Why can't they just let the police handle it?" But just as soon as she had expressed her concern, Stephanie sighed, "I know, we don't have enough concrete evidence to go to the police yet."

"And they certainly haven't done much with our reports," added Jennifer. Then on a positive note she continued, "But don't worry. John's a police officer and I'm sure he'll direct us as to what we should do. We'll probably just watch and see if the guy does anything with the truck and then report his whereabouts." Even as Jennifer tried to ease Stephanie's fears, she wasn't sure she believed it herself. In the back of her mind, she too was concerned and wondered if there was real danger in their plan.

Changing the topic Stephanie gave her a curious look, "So tell me, what was it like marooned on an island all night with a great guy?"

"Actually, I enjoyed his company, and," she smiled, "I felt safe with him." She placed her empty mug beside her plate. "So, I think I will follow his lead and go have a nap for an hour. It looks like it might be a long day."

It was shortly after ten when Jennifer awoke. She lay in bed thinking. The sun had risen past the top of Tyler's cabin and now beamed in her bedroom window reflecting off her dresser mirror. With the cloudless blue sky above, it promised to be a beautiful warm day.

The sound of a vehicle coming down the lodge road prompted her to get up. She wondered if it was Mike returning early then smiled at her excitement as she looked out and saw a black truck approach the office. The Springetts had arrived.

Jennifer could hear Stephanie and the sound of men's voices coming from the office and knew she wouldn't be needed right away so she took the next thirty minutes to shower, wash her hair, and change into clean clothes ready for her working day.

Stephanie was still in the office going over some book work when Jennifer joined her. Stephanie was smiling then closed her book. "Our first fully booked week!" she said.

"That's great!" said Jennifer, happy that things would soon be going well again for her sister.

"Well, what's on your agenda for today?" inquired Stephanie.

"There's not a lot yet. I thought I'd first feed the birds, then check the worm boxes in the tuck shop."

"The laundry's caught up, thanks to our all-nighter," added Stephanie. "And Tyler's here so the garbage is already done, so it looks like you have a free day."

But Jennifer felt like doing something. "What about getting eleven ready for customers," she said eagerly.

"There's no rush. Sam has to make the beds first. Besides you've done a lot since you arrived.
So, you might as well enjoy the day."

"This is going to take some effort but I'll give it a go." Twenty minutes later whirling whizzing humming birds had their feeders filled and seemed to take a revived enthusiasm in the fresh nectar. The tuck shop fridge had been restocked with two dozen worm container boxes and Jennifer now sat on the centre section of the main dock surrounded by sun tanning necessities. Towels, pillow, lotion and as yet unopened "Wilderness Love".

It was unusually quiet. From her vantage point she could see the seven docks of the nearest cottages and all were vacant. There were no children enjoying the sandy beach area or the play area further up the road. The occasional echoing metallic sound came from the boathouse where Jennifer imagined Sam and Tyler were working. There was only the slightest ripple on the water and the silver birch leaves hung undisturbed in the sunlight.

The Springett truck, having been unloaded, now came down the same trail Jennifer had used the day before when she moved Glen and Derek's gear back to number seven. The trail led down past number four and wound past the beach area back to the incoming road and parking area opposite the fish hut. One man walked back from the parked vehicle then paused at the beach area.

"Hi." Jennifer was facing him now, prone on the middle dock laying on her stomach with her hands folded under her chin, her romance novel open to the first page. "Do you have your boat yet?"

He turned now, realizing he had been watched since leaving his truck and stepped up on to the right wing of the dock. "Yes, my brother is speaking with the owner now." His accent betrayed his southern home and he smiled edging closer. "It's a quiet spot."

"Everyone's out on the lake, making up for yesterday I guess." Jennifer sat up now and pulled on her swimsuit cover up. "I hope you like your cottage."

William Springett and his brother James had driven non-stop from Tennessee. Pausing only once to eat, they took turns driving and were now ready to enjoy the next two weeks in the Canadian north. William Springett was tall with what Jennifer surmised was light brown hair under his cowboy hat and brown eyes. He had a slender build and a generous smile. Jennifer guessed by his clothes and leather boots that he hadn't been fishing too often.

The sound of a motor starting up drew their attention to the boathouse. His brother was driving cautiously from the boathouse entrance then giving the dock area a wide berth he waved motioning to his brother to meet him at their dock.

William Springett sat on a cushioned chair near Jennifer now, his leather jacket over his arm, and watched as his brother manoeuvred the boat past the bend then out of sight.

"I'd best be going," he said, a little reluctant to leave the conversation. He noticed Jennifer's gaze at his shirt pocket. The white translucent fabric betrayed its contents and he fished out the red and white package. "I found this in the cottage. Are they yours?"

Jennifer stared at the bullseye trademark on the package of cigarettes, which William Springett now offered her. "No," she said, then reached out and took the opened package, "but I know who they belong to." Jennifer smiled hoping she hadn't betrayed her eagerness to retrieve the package.

Derek Kerr. Had it been him all along? She didn't remember seeing the package when she moved their gear back. Maybe it had been him in cottage twelve spying on her. Eddy probably had been responsible for the truck incidents but had been too afraid to admit it to the police. But how did the key fit in? These thoughts suddenly rushed over her then sensing an awkwardness Jennifer suddenly focused again on the young man before her. "I hope you enjoy your stay."

"Thank you, …Miss?"

"Jennifer."

"Well, Miss Jennifer, I hope we meet again."

She liked the way his southern drawl made her name sound and smiled again as he got up to leave. Jennifer tucked the package under her towel until William Springett had climbed the hill path and was out of sight, then gathered her things before starting back to the office.

Chapter 14

Jennifer hurriedly left the dock eager to share her discovery with her sister. Stephanie was still where Jennifer had left her and looked up with a surprised look when she burst through the door. Throwing her things on an empty chair Jennifer slumped down next to Stephanie. She triumphantly placed the red and white package upright on Stephanie's binder. "This was found in cottage three by Mr. Springett," she said excitedly.

Stephanie stared at the package, "So what are you thinking?"

"It has to be Derek!" she said, emphatically.

"Why Derek?" Stephanie had a puzzled look on her face and couldn't see the connection. Jennifer was forced to explain her reasons now and after a lengthy recount of the pike incident and the two encounters with Derek, Stephanie's look turned from one of disbelief to one of realization. She had come to the same conclusion Jennifer had. "So do you think Eddy actually tampered with the truck?"

"It would make sense, only, the key is the only thing that doesn't fit." She slumped back into her chair. "Unless someone just happened to place a useless key there." But that didn't make a lot of sense. "Maybe kids just playing around? Anyway, Eddy was here when we had the truck trouble."

"So, with Eddy out of the picture, and if it's Derek who's been spying on you, our stake out tonight might just be a waste of time." Stephanie smiled, feeling somewhat relieved now that the danger she had been projecting was minimal.

"Should we tell the guys?"

Stephanie thought for a moment, "Tell them about the package but I think you should leave out the part about Derek."

Jennifer agreed.

The faint sound of a motor revving up could be heard. The Springett brothers were now going out on the lake. Near the bay's sheltering island just before the narrowing passage out to the lake a large somewhat flat rock hovered below the water's surface. It was actually an extension of the island's point with only a third of its top caressing the small waves above the water. Here now the two brothers waited, stranded upon the flat rock.

"That's strange," said Jennifer. "The motor's stopped. I wonder if they're having trouble with it?" Curious Jennifer went outside then waved Stephanie to join her.

From their perspective inside the boathouse entrance, Sam and Tyler had foreseen the accident and now stood on the outer dock and waved at the two brothers bobbing helplessly, their boat's front end resting on the flat rock. "I'll go," offered Tyler.

Jennifer and Stephanie watched from the main dock as Tyler drove over to help detach the boat from the island. Tyler tied a line to the back of their boat. They could see the two brothers both move to the rear of their boat which made the front raise up with just enough clearance so Tyler could pull them backwards without scraping the wooden bottom. Luckily James had thought enough to turn off the motor once he felt them scrape along the rock.

"Do you think it's safe for them to go out on the lake?" asked Jennifer.

"I don't know," confessed Stephanie. "Maybe I should have suggested a guide for their first day."

The sound of a motor in the distance told the girls that someone was returning for lunch. The small lodge boat slowed as it passed through the narrowed passage into the bay revealing Mr. Nelson, John Taylor and the ladies of cottage four. Mr. Nelson slowed their boat to a crawl and took care to skirt the two boats near the island once he saw what was happening. Once safely past he continued his path to the main dock where Jennifer helped guide the boat into a parking space between two buoys.

"Good day," said John Taylor. He smiled as Jennifer took the front rope and tied the boat to the metal loop on the dock. "You're looking chipper after your ordeal."

"A nap helped," replied Jennifer.

After assisting the ladies, Mr. Nelson retrieved his tackle box from the back seat, then as if he suddenly remembered something he addressed Stephanie. "Might we book for supper tomorrow night as well?" he asked.

"Certainly, I'll add your names." Stephanie nodded to the ladies now making their way up the hill. "It looks like you've converted two more."

"They did have a good time today.

"Louisa actually tried my rod," added John Taylor, "and had a fish nibbling at the worm."

John's attention was diverted to the two boats now passing behind them. The Springetts now motored back to their dock as Tyler followed in the guide boat.

The dock swayed up and down as Sam joined them on the dock. He approached Mr. Nelson, who was now carrying his tackle box intending to take it with him to the cottage. "How was your morning?"

157

"Pretty good. I caught two nice pickerel past the narrows and released them." He smiled then glanced towards John Taylor. "John caught ten sunfish, which we released," he emphasized, "and between us all we used three boxes of worms." He shook his head and smiled, "Oh well, we're here to relax and have fun, aren't we?" Sam gave him a pat on the shoulder as Mr. Nelson walked by then followed the ladies up to the cottage.

"I'll be up in a minute, Jeffrey," said John Taylor.

Sam joined the remaining three on the dock. Stephanie gave him a questionable look. "What's happening with the Springetts?" she asked.

"For their own safety Tyler offered to go out with them for an hour, to show them the lake and give them some tips about fishing and how to manoeuvre around the lake." He smiled, "James confessed they've never been on a lake before or in a boat."

Jennifer had been discussing her find with John and now as Sam joined them with Stephanie, Jennifer repeated her discovery, "We found the package of American cigarettes in cottage three. The Springetts found them left on a table."

Sam's eyes widened, "So he was here last night. He must have been watching us the whole time." Sam seemed to be thinking over the matter then addressed John Taylor, "What do you think John, are we still on for tonight?"

"It looks promising. If someone's been here twice, tonight might be the best time to set up watch."

Sam nodded in agreement, "We'll see you at supper then." Jennifer gave Stephanie a conspiratorial glance.

John finished tying up the boat to the rear dock loop then walked with Jennifer as Sam and Stephanie walked back to the office area.

He looked at his new friend then stopped by the coloured chairs at the edge of the beach. "I hope you don't play poker," he started, "you're not very good at keeping secrets." Jennifer smiled awkwardly suddenly aware of his impending interrogation. "So, what else do you know about our intruder?"

Jennifer gave a sigh then fell into one of the coloured chairs. "Just that I think it might be one of the guests, spying on me." Jennifer confided in her ally relating her encounters with Derek.

John Taylor sat next to Jennifer now. He gave her arm a friendly pat. "I don't think we have to worry about Derek," he said. "I'll admit it looks suspicious but I think the key plays a more important part than you're allowing." A dragon fly with iridescent gossamer wings fluttered then landed on the arm of John's chair. "Now isn't that beautiful," he smiled at the small creature who walked along the edge of the red wood as if balancing on a tight rope, then flew away.

Both turned toward the island point as Tyler guided his boat with his two passengers out along its shore. Driving between two bodies of land was usually safer than hugging the shoreline but one still had to always be wary of rocky outcrops.

He slowly demonstrated to the men how to approach an unfamiliar shoreline and what to look for, then drove back into the water way heading out toward the narrows and past the flat gray painted rock, the motor's drone fading as they went.

"Well, I better go before I'm called," said John. "After dinner I think Jeffrey and I are going out again."

Jennifer could hear the enthusiasm in his voice. "I'm glad you're having a good time here. I'll see you at supper."

Sitting still on a hot dock sun tanning wasn't really enjoyable for Jennifer. She would rather be doing something. Maybe a canoe ride. She thought about her first exploration which ended at Mike's cabin. She'd like to see him again but maybe he was still resting. She ran to catch up with Stephanie and Sam.

"I think I'll go for a canoe ride," she said. Not wanting to leave Stephanie to take care of supper alone she asked, "What time are you starting supper?"

Stephanie smiled, up till now Stephanie had forgotten her sister's aversion to sitting still, "Not till three, so you have a while."

She chose the same canoe as she used for her first ride finding it better to handle when paddling alone. It was a beautiful clear day. The sun was high and with no hint of a breeze the intensity of the sun's warmth was more noticeable now. She took the same route as before hugging the shoreline along the deserted lodge property. Even the girls from number eight were absent from their tanning dock and their cottage seemed to be vacant. Jennifer supposed that the girls must have gone to town shopping as the couples had only one boat and it was too small for six people. Jennifer wished now she had brought a sun hat with her. She continued along the shoreline past number eleven and could just see number twelve as she turned the point. The wild rice became more abundant and Jennifer continued to paddle close to shore. She liked to hear the rice as it bent and made a swishing sound as the fiber glass bottom surged forward. Her canoe left a trail of bent stalks as she went.

Around the bend she paddled cautiously careful not to splash the oar and give away her presence. Mike's cabin was visible now and his jeep was parked nearby. She looked around the dock and surrounding beach area. No one. She paddled closer to the sandy shore then hearing nothing she decided to beach her canoe and see if anyone was home.

"Good afternoon!"

Startled, Jennifer turned as her canoe rocked in the shallow water. Mike was in the water on the far side of the dock. He was wet, his hair hanging straight, dripping and his arms were folded as he leaned on the wooden slats.

"Hi," she replied, smiling. She turned her canoe in Mike's direction, intending to join him at the dock. The canoe glided slowly.

"Far enough, Miss Jennifer!" he warned.

From her seat in the canoe Jennifer could now see clothing and a towel at the end of the dock. "Are you skinny dipping?" she asked laughing.

He stood back from the dock then looked down, pretending he hadn't noticed before, then gave her a surprised look. "I guess I am!"

"Well in that case put your suit on then I'll join you."

"You'll have to turn away first," he said, pretending modesty.

"Very well, sir," laughed Jennifer. She back paddled until the canoe was facing the opposite shore and waited. Jennifer could hear splashes and waited dutifully until called to turn back. The splashes sounded closer and just as Jennifer suspected something, her canoe was tugged then tipped just enough to cause her to fall out and land splashing in the shallow water. She screamed just before gulping a mouthful of lake water. Mike was laughing now. The sight of Jennifer sitting on the sandy bottom, her beach robe floating around her neck was priceless.

"Oh, what a picture!" he said, still laughing.

Jennifer released her robe allowing it to float around her. Before it absorbed too much water and sank, she rolled it up and threw it carelessly in the canoe.

The suddenness of her dunking had taken the wind out of her but now sitting on the sandy bottom up to her neck in water, her hair bobbing, caressing her face, she now smiled thinking how she must look.

Mike's look turned from one of amusement to one of regret as he held out his hand. "I'm sorry," he said softly trying not to smile. "Are you all right?"

"Oh, I'm just fine." Jennifer clenched her jaw so she wouldn't smile then reached out to take the offered hand. "But misery does love company." With this said she leaned back bracing her feet in the sandy bottom and gave a pull which threw Mike off balance, then headlong into the water beside her. She laughed at the look on his face as he lost his footing. Once under water Jennifer seized her chance and pounced on the submerged Mike. Mike recovered and tossed her into the warm water. Jennifer splashed back laughing. Mike retaliated

"So, you want a water fight, do you?" and the two ended up splashing each other until they had no more energy. The canoe had drifted toward the dock and was caught up against the uprights at the end. Exhausted the two leaned on each other laughing and giggling at their silliness.

"That was fun," said Jennifer. She took Mike's hand as they trudged through the murky water back to the beach. Together they sat, breathless enjoying the lake view.

"I'll get some towels," offered Mike. He was gone a few minutes then returned with a towel for each of them and one for sitting on. "What a great day!" he exclaimed.

"Now you sound like John Taylor." They laughed.

"It must be interesting for him seeing the north land for the first time. I remember going to Croatia for the first time." Jennifer looked at him with interest as he revealed a little of himself. "But the 'Great Day' feeling didn't last long."

"Anyway, here it is a beautiful day." Jennifer put her arm around his toweled waist. He gave her a hug back and leaned over for a kiss. "Where are they going!" She jumped up waving.

The Springett brothers now on their own were heading steadily towards a small bay to the right of Mike's dock. William saw her and waved. This area Jennifer knew was full of rocks. The brothers made no attempt at slowing down and continued confidently toward the bay.

"Oh, no," she sighed. With their motor running they wouldn't be able to hear a warning so Jennifer could only wave them over hoping they would change course and see what she wanted. Mike joined her attempts yelling for them to stop as well.

Then the sound of metal hitting rock could be heard just as William who was sitting in the front seat of their boat yelled, "Rock!". This time James didn't have a chance to switch off the motor in time. Eventually their boat stopped, perched upon a cluster of rocks that were hidden just below the surface and most likely now, they had damaged the propeller.

"C'mon," said Mike. "Maybe we can help."

It didn't take long for the two of them to retrieve Jennifer's canoe then paddle over to where the two men were stuck. At first William had tried to push themselves off using one of the boat's oars then realized that they had ridden into the rocky trap too far to just back off. James had raised the motor and was now looking at the damaged prop as Jennifer and Mike paddled closer. A large chunk of one blade was missing and one was bent back at the edge. Mike shook his head slowly, "There's a two-hundred-dollar bill," he said.

James nodded in agreement. He looked truly saddened by the damage.

William smiled, embarrassed as Jennifer pulled alongside the lodge boat. "I'll paddle back and get Tyler," she said. "We'll get you off soon."

"It was kind of you to give us a hand. I'm afraid boating isn't one of our strong points." he said.

"Maybe not yet, but you'll learn." She smiled in sympathy at his disappointment. Jennifer wondered how much learning would cost them. "I'll be right back."

Mike had elected to stay with the brothers while Jennifer paddled back to the lodge and took this opportunity to chat with the two newcomers.

The afternoon stayed sunny and bright giving way to only a few wispy clouds in the west. Tyler had arrived with another boat for the two brothers who attempted a further excursion into the wilds of the Canadian north but this time with William at the helm. Although the motor was damaged, Tyler and Mike were eventually able to get the impaired boat back to the lodge on its own steam after first dislodging it from its rocky trap. They moved at a snail's pace with Jennifer out racing them with her canoe but eventually they pulled into the boathouse's inner dock.

Sam greeted the trio at the dock. He knew something had happened to the Springetts' boat but had no idea of the extent of the damage until Tyler tilted up the motor. "Oh boy," was his only comment. The Springetts had passed by the boathouse entrance fifteen minutes earlier and now having heard how the incident had happened Sam was wondering how they would make out for the rest of the day.

"Luckily I have one prop left," he said.

Remembering she had promised to help Stephanie, Jennifer left the two men to repair the motor while she returned the canoe to its wooden rack then went to change into dry clothes.

"That smells good!" she commented after the aroma of roasting beef met her at the kitchen doorway.

"It should," said Stephanie. "That's prime rib roasting away in there." She turned on the oven light so Jennifer could see the size of the roast.

"Sorry I'm late, can I help with the vegetables?"

"Thanks," said Stephanie. "The potatoes are in the sink already but you'll need twelve carrots from the fridge." Stephanie busied herself with the Yorkshire pudding and dessert while Jennifer peeled and cut the remaining vegetables.

"So, what have you been up to that makes you late?" asked Stephanie.

Jennifer laughed, deciding she would relate the Springett episode rather than the water fight.

"Poor Sam, and these boys are staying for two weeks." She laughed at the thought. "Well, it's a good thing we have Tyler."

"How do you want the carrots?" asked Jennifer. "Sliced or strings?"

Jennifer was just finishing up the potatoes and saw Mike and Sam coming to the side kitchen door. She could see the two men smiling and she was glad Mike was there to help Sam. She noticed as Sam was distracted by something and the two abandoned the door and headed down toward the beach area.

Jennifer rinsed her hands and leaving the peeled carrots in the sink went to the dining room door that joined the kitchen, "Something's up."

Stephanie was busy measuring her ingredients for the Yorkshire pudding and took no notice until Jennifer passed her and left the kitchen.

Glen Malloy and Derek were parked at the main dock, a lodge boat rocked gently behind them joined to their stern by a rope that now, slackened off, dipped into the lake.

Jennifer watched as Tyler manned the lodge boat and followed Glen and Derek as they lead the way out of the bay. Mike was laughing and Sam just shook his head.

Jennifer couldn't resist any longer and leaned out the dining room door as the two men approached the lodge steps. "What happened?"

"The Springetts lost their boat," said Mike.

"They what?" said Jennifer, smiling, thinking she hadn't heard correctly.

"Mr. Malloy, found their boat adrift. They searched around a nearby island but no sign of them."

"Could they have fallen overboard?" asked Jennifer, now concerned.

"I doubt that. There was a rope trailing the boat with a large loop at the end. It looks as if they tied the boat to something, probably a large rock and it got away." He shook his head in wonder. "It promises to be a busy week for Tyler."

It was a half hour later that Tyler returned with Glen Malloy and Derek Kerr. The Springett brothers had decided to go exploring on one of the larger islands which was actually part of the mainland that jutted out, and had pulled their boat to the shore. James had tied it to a rock on the shoreline when they got out and the two hadn't even realized their boat had been freed by the coaxing waves until they saw it being towed away, while standing on a rocky outcrop they had climbed further inland.

Chapter 15

Supper that evening was a welcomed rest after an eventful day. John Taylor was seated with the rest of his party at a table for four. The honey moon couple were seated at a table next to Mr. Nelson's party and Rachel was talking to John Taylor's sister about fashion and her latest outfit, while Mr. Newlywed assured Sam again that the water was running perfectly in their cottage.

Tyler had decided to stay, in preparation for the night watch, and was seated with Sam and Mike at a table for six across from the other two parties. Stephanie was serving a slow cooked roast of beef with mashed potatoes and Yorkshire pudding in honour of her British guest. To Jennifer and Mike, it was the most wonderful meal they had ever had.

She sat across from Mike at the table who gave her a sheepish grin while the two of them were being filled in on the evening's events. She gave Tyler a look then smiled and on one of his rare occasions he smiled back knowing now that soon things would be back to normal at the Painted Rock Lodge.

After their sumptuous meal including Stephanie's famous Bavarian creme, Sam brought out liqueurs for everyone. The honeymoon couple who were eager to go out with Tyler again made plans for an early morning start, and Jennifer could see that Tyler no longer felt apart from the lodge family.

The guests slowly departed. The honeymoon couple had a canoe ride planned now that the weather was co-operating. Mr. Nelson who had had his fill of fishing for the day decided a nap after a big meal was the thing for him while the ladies would go back to their cottage and tackle a game of Scrabble.

As his party retired John Taylor joined the others at the table for six and sat next to Jennifer. "What an exciting day this has been," he exclaimed. Then turning to Jennifer, he said, "I didn't get to show you the fish I caught." He held his arms out as part of his description. "It was a pickerel, about this big, and I caught it on father's rod and reel." He smiled from ear to ear. "I'm so glad we figured out the problem with the line. Father will be so happy." He suddenly got excited as if he had forgotten to tell Jennifer the most important news. "Sam said we can take it back home with us, of course there are papers to fill out and I'm sure some kind of cost involved but won't that be wonderful." He gave Tyler a big smile, "Tyler was kind enough to prepare the fish for me. Apparently, you need to keep the skin on so it can be identified."

Jennifer gave his arm a warm squeeze, "I'm so glad," she said.

With all retired, but the six of them in the dining room Sam decided it would be a good time to discuss the evenings events. "John has offered to assist us with tonight's fishing," he smiled. "He was here when the police arrived earlier and knows about our Misha plate discovery." He fingered the key he had taken from his pocket.

"Our first spot," suggested John Taylor, "should be near your truck Sam." Sam nodded in agreement.

"What about the road coming into the lodge?" asked Stephanie.

"We know he's been hiding out in number twelve,"

offered Jennifer, "maybe we should be watching there too."

It took almost an hour for the six to plan their watch. After two failed attempts their intruder would be getting desperate by now. Maybe nothing would happen but if it did, they were sure by the way they had staked out the lodge grounds that nothing would go unnoticed. Sam had a pair of walkie-talkies that Tyler and John would have in cottage number eleven knowing that their intruder had stayed for a while in number twelve. Mike and Jennifer would be situated in the fish cleaning hut, not a pleasant spot but the road leading up to the lodge could be observed as well as the truck itself.

Stephanie would remain in the office area with the second walkie-talkie and watch for any guests that might need assistance and detract them from the truck area while Sam would sit in Tyler's cabin directly across from the truck. Because the communication devices made a noise Stephanie wrapped hers in a blanket. If she heard from Tyler, she would flick the lights on and off as a signal to the others that their intruder was coming from the other end of the lodge.

It was hot in the fish hut. There were only two small windows and no place to sit. The remains of recently cleaned fish were in the closed garbage can under the wooden counter but Jennifer could still smell the odour left by the guts and heads. The door to the hut was screened and with the light off their presence would be unnoticed by anyone walking by.

Across from them and up the road a little was the guest parking area, a place where after leaving any boat trailers up on the hill, guests could safely park their vehicles away from the cottage and beach area. The winding drone of a motor told them that one of the fishing boats was coming back to the lodge for the night. A fly buzzed around the hut searching for the leftovers. Mike swatted it away. The hut was fairly small and Mike enjoyed the opportunity to be with Jennifer in these tight premises. He took her hand and gently tugged her towards him. "Not exactly the kind of place I'd bring you for our third date," he whispered.

"Oh, I don't know. It's actually quite romantic in its own way. Natural wood interior, running water, air conditioning." She directed her arms accordingly to embellish the huts features then swatted away a mosquito that buzzed around her face. Mike stifled a laugh. He leaned down to kiss her, his arms now around her pulling her closer, then he noticed it.

Across from them in the car park area, a faded blue Chrysler was parked next to a Volkswagen. It had been backed in and was on the fringe of the parking area too close to the saplings and shrubs that brushed the passenger side door. "Jen, look!" Ready for the kiss that didn't happen Jennifer turned wondering what Mike was looking at. "Does that car look familiar to you?"

"I'm not sure." She stared at the car through the screen. "No, wait," she thought back to her first day here, her first truck experience, "I think it's like the one that forced me off the road! I remember the peeling clear coat on the hood"

Mike noticed something else, "It has U.S. plates too!"

Jennifer felt a shiver go through her. It wasn't Derek after all. Everything was clear now. The same person responsible for running her off the road was here now at the lodge. This was his car and she knew now that he wanted the key.

Abandoning romance for the moment Mike looked around slowly. There was no one nearby. Children's voices could be heard from the beach as they splashed and played with the water toys in the shallow roped off area. "We have to tell the others," he whispered.

"What if he saw us come in here? Won't he wonder why we've been in here with no fish and suspect something?"

"If he saw us, yes." He thought for a moment, "Maybe he's nearby waiting for us to leave. So just in case let's give him a show."

From inside Tyler's cabin Sam could hear them leaving the fish hut. Jennifer was giggling and Mike held her hand. As they walked, he would occasionally pull her toward him and give her a quick kiss. They hugged on the steps of Tyler's cabin and as Jennifer stretched up to put her arms around Mike she whispered through the screen door, "Sam, he's here! His car is over there!"

She giggled again, and teasingly pulled away from Mike and made her way over to the office, leaving Mike to walk alone down to the boathouse. She would tell Stephanie who would radio her message to the other blanketed receiver.

The sun was low in the sky now and in less than a half hour it would be dark. Before Jennifer got to the office door, she could hear a muffled conversation. To any one passing by it might sound like a radio programme but Jennifer knew it was Tyler. Stephanie flicked the lights. Jennifer ran down the path in front of the dining room windows. She waved to Stephanie as she passed then caught up to Mike. She took him by the hand then snuggled closer so she could whisper. "Tyler just called Stephanie."

"In here!" Together they ducked into the boathouse hoping no one had seen them. Keeping to the shadows they waited near the entrance. A dry branch snapped outside the boathouse entrance. Someone was coming. Jennifer could hear the footsteps and rattle of a metal can's dangling cap and chain. She quickly went to the fridge pretending to check the boxes of worms.

Derek Kerr smiled when he saw Jennifer standing alone by the fridge then noticed Mike to the right of the opening choosing a tool from the rack that hung above the bench. "Hi," he said, a disappointed look on his face. "I came to get another tank of gas."

He glanced at Mike, then helped himself to a tank from the shelf labelled guests tanks, exchanging it with his empty tank.

"I'll check you out," offered Jennifer. On a clipboard tied to the shelf, Jennifer wrote down Derek's name, the date and the new gas tank number. "There," she smiled.

Derek had been watching her fill in the information as Mike left the bench to wait for Jennifer outside. His mood seemed to brighten now with Mike's absence. "I'm not doing anything later tonight." He switched to one of his relaxed poses as he leaned against the tool bench then suggested, "Maybe we could get together."

"I don't think so," then glancing to see if Mike was outside, she added in a whisper, "my fiancée probably wouldn't like it."

Derek straightened abruptly, as if all of a sudden he remembered he had to hurry back. Picking up the gas can he nodded in acknowledgement of the situation and left.

Jennifer tried not to laugh at his awkward expression and just watched with faked wide-eyed innocence as he passed Mike in silence on his way back to number seven.

"What was all that about?" asked Mike once he was back in the shadow of the boathouse.

Jennifer gave him a smirk, "Oh, he just wanted a date."

"Well. I'm glad you got rid of him. We don't have much time." Mike had been watching Stephanie from the side window of the dining room. She had waved and pointed to her watch several times while Mike was waiting for Derek to move on.

"What do we do if he's got a gun?" Jennifer was starting to wonder what they would do if they caught the intruder searching the truck. Suddenly she had second thoughts about this stake out.

Mike looked at her. She could see him thinking. He picked up a pair of pliers and a screwdriver off the tool table. "Come on, I've got an idea!" Together they raced back across the dining room windows and back up towards the fish hut. Passing the fish hut Mike went directly over to the blue car. "Keep watch," he said. One by one he flattened the back tires. The windows were rolled down and there was a two-foot-long scrape along the driver side door. Mike opened the door carefully and just as the intruder had sabotaged Sam's truck, he used the pliers to cut the wires below the dash.

"There," he said, "he won't be going far in that car. But if he decides to use force, we're in trouble." Meeting

Jen at the front of the car together they rushed back to the fish hut and waited.

It was still light when John Taylor saw a figure lurking in the woods around number twelve. "Tyler, look over there!" Tyler left the bedroom window guarding the side of the cottage facing the path and joined John Taylor in the living room to look out the window facing number twelve. Their intruder was lighting up a cigarette just outside cottage twelve then went inside out of view of the two hidden men. Tyler contacted Stephanie then the two just waited.

Light from the setting sun poured into the lake side windows and the two sat on the north side of the room by John Taylor's window careful not to create shadows that might be seen. John Taylor had been on several surveillance operations early in his career and this reminded him of those days in the force. "I'd forgotten the excitement of staking out a location," he smiled, "but I suppose one tends to remember the exciting moments like now when you have the subject in your sites."

What they would do if the intruder tried to come into their cottage, they didn't know but Tyler had taken the precaution of locking the door from the inside just in case. "He probably won't attempt anything until dark," offered Tyler. "Once he leaves, we can follow at a safe distance along the lake."

Dusk turned into dark and it was nearly nine o'clock before he left number twelve. He skulked along the path, constantly glancing in all directions as he went. Mosquitoes, disturbed from their hiding place in leafy plants along the path buzzed up in clouds as he walked along. Once he had been seen by a couple near their dock but they had just nodded a friendly, "Good evening." He felt tonight was his last chance. They must have seen the truck by now. He had thoroughly searched the interior and undercarriage looking for any hiding place his partner might have used. He had failed in his attempts to isolate the vehicle so tonight whether he had to use force or not he would check the exterior and engine. He had to have that key.

Since the sun went down the night air became cooler which was a welcome relief to Jennifer and Mike. Fishermen had returned now and all the lodge boats were accounted for. Luckily no one had the need to use the fish hut leaving Jennifer and Mike undetected in their hiding spot. They had been in the fish hut a little over an hour waiting and listening.

A car came up the lodge road. It slowly moved past the fish hut and parked outside the office window, perhaps people were just enquiring as to available accommodations. Jennifer and Mike watched as two men got out and followed the office sign to the steps leading inside. Stephanie greeted them at the door and the three went into the small office attached to the porch. They were both tall men dressed in jeans and light jackets. The driver, probably the older of the two sported a full moustache and a baseball cap. The second man was slimmer and his short blonde hair shone in the porch light.

Jennifer wanted to go out and help Stephanie but Mike convinced her that keeping their hiding spot was more important.

Sam had been alone in Tyler's cabin for quite a while. He had had time to think and was beginning to have second thoughts about their plan. Was confronting the intruder really a good idea. He had his rifle, but would he actually use it if things got nasty. He wasn't sure, he wasn't sure of anything now.

Tyler and John had left their cottage. They could see him now as he passed through the light shone from the boathouse onto the dock. He was taking the back path the one closest to the truck area.

From his vantage point the intruder could see shadows of people on the dining room curtains. He hoped most of the lodge staff was inside leaving him free to wander behind the lodge. During his walk from the far cottage, he had played different scenarios in his mind. Searching the engine would make more noise than he wanted and surely someone would hear him. He needed more time. He needed the truck, and up till now had searched it during short opportune moments. He now realized what he needed to do and why he hadn't thought of it before annoyed him. The phone wires were running down the back side of the lodge close to the truck. He would cut those before hot wiring the truck. By tomorrow morning he would have the time he needed to search properly. It meant leaving his car and picking up another but he didn't

177

mind, stealing another vehicle wouldn't be hard. Getting back across the border might be a little difficult but he'd done it before and wasn't worried.

Determined now with his plan worked out in his head the intruder quickened his steps past the end window. He was at the back of the lodge now. It was dark and he was confident no one had seen him. Ducking down below the windows he hurried along the length of the lodge to the wires. He smiled to himself picturing the look on their faces when they found out they couldn't call the police.

Mike thought he saw something move in the shadows. It was dark behind the lodge so he wasn't sure. Jennifer was keeping watch out of the screen door. She had already brushed away two mosquitoes and a spider from her face during their stake out and jumped slightly when Mike touched her arm.

Moving over to his window she saw where he was pointing. Someone was reaching up. They heard the snip as the wire was cut then the figure dropped down along the side of the building. He paused when he heard the dining room door open and close and remained motionless for several minutes waiting until he could hear conversation again.

Sam had seen all of this from his vantage point across from the truck. He sat in a chair in the darkness by the screen door wondering when he should make a move toward this man who now crouched down near his truck and didn't move.

"What should we do?" whispered Jennifer.

"I'm not sure." confessed Mike. "He's cut the phone wire." He looked at Jennifer, her eyes shining in the dark. "Do you have a cell phone?"

"Yes, in my car." Mike winced at the glitch in his plan.

"We had a good dress rehearsal, are you up for the live performance?"

Jennifer's eyes widened. "You mean, go out there past him holding hands, then get the phone from my car and call the police?"

"Something like that," he nodded back.

"One problem," she whispered, "the car's locked and the keys are in my room." Mike slumped back against the wall of the hut.

Tyler and John Taylor had entered the dining room from the dock side and were now filling Stephanie in on the progress of the intruder. Jennifer heard a familiar voice and was confused by it. "Listen," she whispered.

"Good night, see you early tomorrow, Tyler," called John Taylor. They could see John Taylor as he walked by the dock path and up to his cottage on the hill. The flood light casting shadows as he walked past the shrubs that lined the trail.

The figure behind the lodge moved as if startled then shrunk back to his previous position.

Sam had heard the evening departure as well but stayed where he was. He was watching, watching as the man now moved toward his truck. He had his rifle, he thought Mike and Jennifer would hear him and their presence would pressure the intruder to give up. He decided. He would step out and call for the man to raise his hands.

"Stop! Hands up!"

"This is the police!" shouted a second man.

Jennifer and Mike could see them clearly now. The two men who had stopped at the office were now on either side of the intruder, their guns raised and pointing at the man who was now standing erect with his hands up. The man with the moustache cuffed their suspect while the man with the short blonde hair searched for a weapon.

Relieved, Sam set down his rifle and came out of Tyler's cabin. He was immediately joined by Stephanie who with Tyler had been waiting inside the office as instructed by the police. "I'm glad this is over Sam," and she gave him a big hug.

It was now that Mike let Jennifer safely join the others by the truck. Watching from his cottage window, John Taylor now hurried down the path to the dock followed by a confused Mr. Nelson and the two ladies. "Well done, Gentlemen, well done," he said.

Sensing a familiarity between John Taylor and the police officers Jennifer eased over to stand next to John. "What's going on," she whispered.

As they had promised Stephanie, the two officers prepared to leave the lodge discreetly. Sam reached into his pants pocket, "You might want to take this with you." When he saw the key, the cuffed man tried to lunge toward Sam then was pulled back as he was instructed to get into the car.

A few of the cottagers who had heard the police warning stood around the plain looking car as the suspect was helped into the back seat. Glen Malloy and Derek Kerr were walking up the back path toward the truck curious about all the commotion. Feeling the need to give them some explanation Sam called to the gathering guests, "Just someone trying to steal my truck," he said. "It's all been taken care of now. Good night!" He leaned a little on Stephanie, his arm around her. It had been a very long day.

Stephanie couldn't wait to tell the stake out team what had happened. "Let's all go inside," she suggested. "I don't know about you, but I need something chocolate after that!"

Chocolate cake made for tomorrow's supper hit the spot and between bites Stephanie explained how she had called the police after Tyler had called her on the walkie-talkie about the intruder. She had seen Derek at the boathouse and knew now that there was a far more dangerous man stalking the lodge. "I'm sorry," she explained, "but I didn't want anyone to get hurt."

The six sat around the dining room table enjoying the aftermath of a suspenseful evening. A pitcher of coffee hissed its readiness as Jennifer offered refills, "I don't get it," she said after pouring Mike another cup, "if you knew the police were coming why didn't you tell us?"

"It was too late," explained Stephanie, "Tyler and John knew once they came back to the lodge, but I couldn't tell you without frightening him away."

After their earlier visit the police had been cautioned about this possible killer. Reports from their counterparts in the States warned that he had crossed the border and with the vehicle description and possible location given to them by the license bureau worker Mary Willis, they had been watching and waiting for a sign of him since last week. Sam's report about mysterious incidents involving his truck along with the MISHA plate had given them further hopes of apprehending this fugitive.

"What about the key?" asked Sam. "Did they say why he wanted it so badly?"

"I can answer that," said John Taylor. "I spoke with the one gentleman while you were giving your statements. According to the American police this fellow was wanted for the murder of his former partner, a garage owner."

"Renson?" said Sam, "Where I took my truck?"

"Yes," confirmed John. "The two had stolen some counterfeit plates and when our man got out of jail his buddy, Renson, refused to tell him where they were, hoping to sell them, I suppose."

Mike who was enjoying the conversation and the chance to sit down and relax after a stressful day, couldn't resist, "And I bet he locked them up somewhere and hid the key."

"Very good," smiled John. "It shouldn't take them long to find out where. We have our ways of finding out these things you know," he smiled confidingly. "Well, I'm off now. I'm sure Louisa and the Nelson's are wondering what has become of me." As he rose to get up, he extended his hand to Tyler, "Very nice working with you, delightful time! Good night, all."

As he left, Tyler remembering the honeymoon couple, also dismissed himself from the group, "I have an early morning fishing date, Boss. See you all tomorrow." He gave Jennifer a look and then a smile, "I'm glad things will be back to normal now. Good night."

Sam's gaze followed Tyler as he left, "I'm glad things

worked out alright for Tyler. I'm not sure what will happen to Eddy but we shouldn't have any more unusual incidents now."

"I don't know," sighed Jennifer. "This has been the most exciting vacation I have ever had. I think I'm going to miss it. Without saboteurs and killers messing up things what ever will I do with my day?"

"Well for starters, the Springetts will need some babysitting," offered Stephanie.

"And don't forget the garbage," teased Sam, "Tyler will be out on the lake all day."

"Then there's supper for eight later," added Stephanie smiling.

"Okay, okay, maybe I will find enough to do."

"And I don't suppose your evenings will be too dull," Stephanie gave Mike a knowing look and smile as she got up to clear away the table.

Mike smiled and gave her a wink. "Speaking of evenings, it's not midnight yet, what about relaxing out on the dock under the stars and let these two get some rest."

"Sounds … exciting." laughed Jennifer.

It was just after midnight when the boathouse spotlight turned itself off. Jennifer and Mike had been sitting in the dark side by side in two of the colourful lodge chairs. The waves gently meandered up to the edge of their shoes teasingly then back out again in a rhythmic manner. Froth made by the days earlier gusting wind still hugged the water line and floated back and forth as the water advanced and receded. The sky was clear now and the moon above them reflected speckles of light across the lake. They held hands and gazed up at the night sky, counting together every time they saw a shooting star.

Every third sighting Jennifer would giggle in a whisper as Mike leaned over and kissed her.

"This is very pleasant, Miss Jennifer."

His hand was warm in hers and reassuring and at that moment she felt she could stay like this forever. The evening air was getting damp and Jennifer felt a shiver go through her. "Is there room for two on that chair?" she hinted.

"Just enough," he smiled.

Jennifer pulled her long hair back and nestled in next to him her face resting on his chest. His arms closed around her.

"I forgot; I've got some more news for you."

"Does it have to do with motors, keys, or fish huts?" she enquired, then laughed.

"As a matter of fact, there is a key involved." Mike fished into his jean pocket and pulled out a key on a thin brass coloured chain, then showed it to Jennifer.

Interested now, Jennifer sat up and stared at the key glinting in the moon light.

"My friend sold the cabin I'm staying in. The new owner gets possession of this key Friday."

"So that means you only have this week left. Oh, Mike!" She gave him a warm hug.

"Actually, only three days left to rent the cabin."

He put his hand under her chin and gently lifted her face up so he could see her better. He leaned over his lips brushing against hers then engulfing them in a passionate kiss. She hugged him again.

"Then after that I own it forever." He smiled at his little masquerade, then laughed as he saw her expression.

"Oh, Mike, that's wonderful," and they kissed again under another shooting star

Jacqueline Opresnik lives in Ontario, Canada, with her husband Frank and Bengal cat, Tiggy. She received her degree in mathematics and geology from Brock University. She earned her pilot's licence shortly after, where she met her husband. Jackie pursued a teaching career and taught in the Elementary grades.

She has had a love of writing since she was ten and is just now beginning to fulfill her dreams as an author. Jackie has spent several years researching her family history and has used many of those finds as inspiration for her novels.